Books by Joy Nash

The Nephilim Series
Demons and Angels (2017)
The Night Everything Fell Apart

Druids of Avalon Series
Celtic Fire
The Grail King
Deep Magic
Silver Silence

Immortals Series
The Awakening
The Crossing
Blood Debt

also by Joy Nash
A Little Light Magic
Christmas Unplugged
Looking for a Hero

www.joynash.com
extras, excerpts
behind the book secrets

Praise for Joy Nash

Silver Silence

"Spellbinding! Joy Nash combines her knowledge of Celtic lore with timeless legends and writes breathtaking romance of unconditional love amid a backdrop of lush descriptions and powerful magic." ~*Paranormal Romance Reviews*

The Grail King

A Romantic Times TOP PICK! "Not since Mary Stewart's *Merlin Trilogy* has the magic of Avalon flowed as lyrically off the pages." ~*RT BOOKreviews Magazine*

A Little Light Magic

"One of those books that when you finish reading it, you have to turn around and start it all over again." ~*Bitten by Books*

The Crossing

"Splendidly entertaining." ~*Booklist* on *The Crossing*
"Mac's personality is in full blaze. It is impossible not to fall in love with this man!" ~*Romance Junkies*

Looking for a Hero

"Oh man! A hilarious ride that had me falling out of my seat with laughter... Don't miss this story." ~*Romance Reviews Today*

Christmas Unplugged

Joy Nash

JOYNASH BOOKS LLC
Doylestown PA

Christmas Unplugged
Copyright © 2013 by Joy Nash
ISBN 978-1941017005
Published by: joynash books, llc
Doylestown PA, USA
Cover design by StoryWonk
Interior design by Joy Nash
Looking for a Hero
Copyright © 2013 by Joy Nash

First Paperback Edition: October 2016

To my mother,
who loved Christmas

Chapter One

The computer screen went dark.

Casey blinked, head jerking up, brain blanking, her elbow smacking an almost-empty coffee mug. It disappeared over the edge of the desk with a crash.

"Looking for this?" a sweet voice asked.

"Damn it, Emma." Casey snatched up the mug, eyeing the dark splashes on the carpet. "Look what you made me do."

"Me?" Emma laughed. "That mug was already hanging on the edge. I'm not even sure what law of gravity was keeping it up."

Casey eyed the computer plug dangling from her sister's French manicured fingertips. "Whatever. Just plug that thing back in, okay? I'm busy."

Emma swung the cord like a lasso. "Oh, really? Doing what?"

"Working."

Emma's brown eyes widened. "So you're a professional candy crusher now? I had no idea."

Casey blew a strand of hair out of her eyes. "Just. Plug. It. In."

"No. Not until we talk. I hate competing with your electronics."

A flicker of real hurt showed in Emma's eyes. Casey inhaled a vague stab of guilt. Em's hair wasn't done, and she was wearing her old community college drama club sweatshirt. The one with "Chicago" on the front and a list of cast members on the back, Em's name at the top. The thing was so ratty a homeless rag picker would roll his shopping cart right over it.

"Something's wrong," she said. "You didn't get that audition you wanted so badly, did you? But so what? It's a Broadway production. You knew just getting in the door would be a long shot."

A very long shot. A minimum distance of about a dozen light years, in Casey's private opinion. Sure, Emma was a decent actress, with the looks of a beauty pageant contestant, but this was New York, for chrissakes, not Broward County. It was Broadway theater, not center stage at a South Florida community college.

There had to be a zillion aspiring actresses with Emma's looks and talent in the city. Most of them, including Emma, were waiting tables. But Casey's star-struck sister was ever hopeful. Casey tried hard to keep her skepticism at a low boil.

"No, I didn't get in," Emma sighed. "But then, I didn't really expect to. I don't know the right people yet."

"Then what's with the sweatshirt?"

Emma sank down on Casey's bed, dropping the computer cord on the floor. "Oh, Case, it's over. Me and

Todd." She made an angry sound in her throat, and Casey could almost see the steam coming out her ears. "I caught him with his tongue down Ashley's throat! Can you believe it? There I was, covering three of the jerk's tables, along with all of my own, while he was getting hot in the walk-in freezer!"

"Hope you told the maître-d'," Casey muttered, eyeing her computer's lifeline, lying on the rug an inch beyond the tapping toe of Emma's pink Prada sneakers.

"You bet I did," Emma shot back. "She was on Todd's balls in two seconds flat."

"Fired?"

"Yep. Ashley, too."

"Good. So forget the loser. You can do better."

"Oh, I know that."

Casey hid a smile. Her little sister was nothing, if not confident. And not without reason. Emma was blonde and beautiful, with a Barbie-doll figure that caused men to drool and women to turn green. She was never single for long.

Casey leaned over and picked up the computer cord. She really needed to think about getting a back-up power system.

"I guess it's all for the best, really," Emma went on. "Now we can spend the holiday together. Honestly. I never should have booked that Adirondack Christmas weekend in the first place. What was I thinking? Why didn't you talk me out of it?"

The trouble was, Casey thought wryly, that Emma

didn't think. Ever. She acted on impulse, and Casey could rarely talk her out of anything. Emma's sudden Christmas plans had caught Casey by surprise, to say the least. She'd been a little hurt at first—this was their first Christmas in New York, after all, and Casey had assumed they'd spend it together. But after some thought, she'd decided she really didn't mind the prospect of skipping Christmas. She had a lot of work to do between now and New Year's Eve.

But now it looked like Christmas was back on. Casey, plug in hand, dropped to her knees and reached sideways into the dark space between her desk and the filing cabinet. The electrical outlet was back there. Somewhere.

"That's great," she said. "We can go uptown, maybe see the big Christmas tree at Rockefeller Center."

"Well, I suppose we could drive by the tree on our way out of the city."

Casey twisted her head to look at her sister. "What do you mean, on our way out of the city? What are you talking about?"

"The Adirondacks," Emma said with exaggerated patience. "Hello? Weren't we just talking about this?"

Casey sat back on her heels. "You mean you still want to go to the Adirondacks? With me instead of Todd? Oh, no. No way."

"Why not? It'll be fun."

"Fun?" Casey repeated. "Fun? Are you nuts? What it'll be is cold. Freezing. Forget it. Just cancel the hotel and get your money back."

"But I can't. It's a small family-run lodge, not a hotel.

A special holiday deal, no refunds. And, Case, I really was looking forward to it. It'll be so pretty. Like Christmas in the movies. Do you realize there's already snow in Dutch Gorge? Probably more than either of us have ever seen in our lives."

"And that's way more than I ever want to see. I was perfectly fine with South Florida Christmases."

It hadn't been her idea, after all, to migrate north. It had been another of Emma's harebrained schemes—go to New York and become famous. Casey could hardly let her little sister launch herself on the New York theater scene without backup. Emma was barely twenty-two, without a penny in the bank, and an erratic work history. She couldn't afford to rent a roach-infested broom closet in this city.

"Oh come on," Emma wheedled. "It's not like you're doing anything this weekend anyway."

Casey finally united cord and outlet. She pushed to her feet as the blessed squeal of computer start-up began. "Not doing anything? Emma, are you insane? I've got to get an interactive billboard on Times Square linked up with three social networks by New Year's Eve."

"Oh, right. But Case, your boss can't possibly expect you to work over Christmas weekend!"

"Wanna bet?"

"That's criminal. What kind of Scrooge do you work for, anyway? You've been at it night and day for weeks as it is! For heaven's sakes, you're not a machine. You need to unplug for a couple days. And it'll be good for us to get away together. We hardly even see each other anymore."

That was true enough. Since they'd moved to New York last spring, Emma had spent every spare minute tracking down potential casting calls and networking with other wannabe actors, while Casey had worked about a zillion hours of overtime at her job as a computer programmer for an interactive marketing agency.

"We hardly need to go to the frozen back of beyond to spend time together," Casey said. "I can grab a few hours this weekend, and we can catch a play or something."

Emma grimaced. "Please. I need a break from the business. I need to get out of Manhattan for a few days. But I really don't want to go alone. Please say you'll come with me? Please?"

Casey's resolve wavered. "Damn it, Emma, why couldn't you have bought a trip to Jamaica?"

"Because it's Christmas! I want a winter wonderland. You know, like in the movies. Snow. Ice skating. Chestnuts roasting on an open fire. Come on, Casey, say you'll come. It's only four days. Dutch Gorge is...well, it's kind of off the beaten trail. If I had to find it on my own..."

The thought of Emma lost in a rented car on some mountain back road sent a chill down Casey's spine. To put it mildly, her sister and road maps didn't mix. Even with a GPS, she couldn't find her way out of a cardboard box. Casey did some hasty mental calculating. She could probably spare the time to drive upstate.

"Oh, all right. My team's pretty much on schedule with the Times Square deadline. If Aiden and Raj can cover for me, I should be able to take the weekend off. But you can forget about seeing me in ice skates. I'm bringing my laptop, and staying inside."

"Your laptop? Um, Casey, do you really think you'll need it?"

"Yes. I really do. Don't argue with me on this one, Emma. I need to put in at least twenty hours between now and Sunday."

Emma bit her lip, and, for a moment, looked as if she was about say something else. Then she shrugged. "All right, go ahead and bring your computer. I don't mind."

Chapter Two

Emma peered through the windshield. "The turn-off to Dutch Gorge is coming up. Soon, I think."

"You're not sure?"

"Well, no..."

Casey sighed and kept driving. The narrow country road cut tight arcs through a forest of graceful white birch trees. The falling snow made things even more picturesque.

It was pretty, she supposed. Even if the rent-a-wreck subcompact car reeked of cigarette smoke. Even if Casey's phone had lost its GPS signal five miles of mountain road ago. Even if Casey had less than no experience driving on snow. Were you supposed to turn into a skid, or out of it? She could never remember.

Emma's blond hair fell forward as she studied the tiny map on the Dutch Gorge Lodge brochure. "Actually, I think we might have already passed the turn-off. It's hard to tell by this tiny map in the brochure."

The last thread of Casey's patience snapped. She hit the brakes...and felt her back tires slip to the left. She jerked the steering wheel in the same direction.

Thank God. She'd guessed right. Somehow, she managed slide to a stop without pitching headlights-first into the drainage chasm that ran alongside the road.

She snatched the resort brochure from Emma's fingers. "Here. Let me see that thing. All I need is for it to get dark, and I'll never find the damn place. Geez. You might have told me Dutch Gorge was in the middle of freaking nowhere! Any farther north, we'd be chasing down Canadian Mounties."

Emma sniffed. "But you have to admit, the snow is pretty."

"Yeah. Pretty damn dangerous."

Casey glared at the location diagram. Even as sketchy as it was, it was obvious they'd gone too far. Shoving the brochure back at Emma, she executed a slippery three-point turn. The snow—the beautiful, dangerous snow—was coming down in big heavy flakes. Casey switched on the windshield wipers and prayed she stayed on the pavement.

If they hadn't been so far from the state highway, she could have turned back. But the last town they'd passed had been miles and miles ago, and night wasn't far off. There was no way she'd make it back to civilization before dark. Surely they couldn't be more than a mile or two from Dutch Lodge. She squinted through the white.

"Finally."

The turn-off was barely paved, and all but unnoticeable. Casey made the left, her muffler scraping ice as the rental car bounced in and out of a frozen rut.

"Lovely," she muttered.

From there, it was all downhill. Literally. Steeply. Apparently, the "Gorge" part of Dutch Gorge Lodge wasn't a fanciful marketing ploy.

She felt like she was descending into some kind of icy version of hell. At least the potholes provided some traction. And the series of hairpin switchbacks ensured she didn't fall asleep at the wheel.

"Oh. My. God," Emma breathed, one hand braced on the dashboard, the other clutching the side of Casey's headrest. "We're going to die."

"And to think," Casey said through gritted teeth, "we could've died in Jamaica. Lying on the beach. Drinking piña coladas. Why in God's name didn't you book a trip to the Caribbean?"

"Todd wanted to." Emma's voice trembled. "But I wanted a romantic white Christmas."

"You got the white part at least."

There were a couple of sniffs, and a discreet swipe of a glove to Emma's eyes. Casey, however, was in no mood to offer sympathy. Maybe later, when—*if*—they arrived alive.

Casey's knuckles had gone white. Her thumbs were numb. She might have turned around, if the damn road had been wide enough. Or backed up, if the damn road hadn't been so steep. As it was, they were in for one long, terrifying slide.

She rode the brake, inching forward as quickly as she dared through snow-dusted evergreens, the afternoon light fading far more quickly than she would have liked.

She prayed the road leveled out before her nerves completely snapped.

"This had better be the right road. There had better be a lodge at the end of it. Because by the time we get to the bottom of this hellish ditch, it's going to be too dark to climb back out. They won't find our cold, dead corpses until spring."

Her sister sniffed. "Don't be ridiculous."

Blood pounded in Casey's ears. Her head, she was sure, was two seconds from exploding. "Ridiculous? Me? Look in the mirror, why don't you? Do you even have two brain cells to rub together? This has got to be your stupidest idea yet."

"It wasn't stupid!"

"It was! It's another one of your half-baked schemes. Bad enough you were going to drag that loser Todd all the way up here. He deserved it. But did you have to drag me into this fiasco?"

"Well." *Sniff.* "I'm sorry you feel so bad about— "*Sniff.* "—celebrating Christmas with your only sister. Your *heartbroken* only sister."

"Oh please, Todd isn't worth a single tear, let alone a broken heart. I'm just sorry he wasn't the one who paid for this trip in advance."

"Well, me too."

The road suddenly dipped, taking Casey's stomach with it. The car skidded for a good hundred feet before regaining traction on another hard bump. Casey wondered if her heartbeat would ever regain a normal rhythm.

"Damn it, Em! Couldn't you have at least rented an SUV instead of this death trap?"

"Excuse me for trying to save money! Anyway, there's no use complaining about it now. It's too late to go back up that mountain. We're committed."

"Oh, one of us should be committed," Casey said darkly. "I just don't know if it's you or me. How the hell did you find out about this place, anyway?"

"There was an ad in that free newspaper they give out all over the city."

"And just what, exactly, did it say?"

Emma half-turned toward the passenger window. "Something like...Get away from it all. Enjoy a romantic old fashioned Christmas."

"Lovely," Casey said again, grinding her teeth. A sharp pain shot through her jaw.

The paved road, such as it was, ended. Casey's wheels skidded on gravel. The snow-dusted evergreen boughs seemed to part before her, as if revealing some long-held secret.

Some secret. A small, snow-slicked parking area occupied by a battered pick-up truck and five SUVs.

"There's no sign." Casey scanned the parking area and the old stone farmhouse on the other side.

"No, but this is definitely the place," Emma replied on a long exhale. She waved the brochure photo. "See?"

The car slid down the last few feet of road. Too fast. Casey hit the brakes. Too hard. The car went into a wide, taillight-first spin.

"Oh, shit!"

The back tires hit a mound of snow. Casey's head thumped against the headrest. She jerked on the steering wheel, but the front wheels kept sliding.

They hit the snow bank, Casey's right front fender kissing the back bumper of a massive black SUV with Massachusetts plates.

"Thank God," Emma breathed.

Cautiously, Casey turned the wheel to the left and eased her foot onto the accelerator. Her tires spun. She gunned the motor harder. The tires spun some more.

"That's it," she said. "The end of traction as we know it. This rotten excuse for a vehicle isn't traveling another inch. At least not tonight." She sighed and opened her door.

To a blast of frigid winter wind.

Once again, lovely.

"Damn, it's cold." She hopped from one foot to the other as she fished her gloves out of her coat pockets.

On the other side of the car, Emma hiked her fur-lined hood up over her head. "But it's so beautiful."

It *was* pretty, Casey had to admit. Even—especially— in the falling snow. Like a Christmas card. The slate-roofed farmhouse stood framed by a steep wooded hill, smoke curling from one of its three chimneys. A covered porch sheltered a large bay window, softly glowing. A huge old tree, its leafless branches painted white with snow, spread its arms over the attic dormers. An old stone well adorned the front yard, and Casey could just make out the outline of a red barn behind the house.

"Look," Emma said suddenly, clutching Casey's arm.

"Emma. I've got to get the luggage—"

"Forget the luggage! Just *look*."

Casey looked. Two men had rounded a corner of the farmhouse, arms laden with firewood. Casey watched as they added the logs to a stack in a lean-to near the porch.

"Yeah?" she said. "So?"

"So? Ohmygod! Did you get a look at those guys?" Emma waved a hand. "Yoohoo! Hi!"

The men looked toward Emma, then back at each other. Casey thought they exchanged a few words before dumping the rest of their firewood and starting across the snow-covered yard.

"Oh. My. God," Emma breathed again. "They're even better looking up close. That tall one is gorgeous."

He was. Tall, muscular and hatless, with enticing, snow-dusted brown hair. Also, as far as she could tell, ridiculously handsome. Around thirty, Casey guessed. His long legs, encased in faded jeans, ended at battered tan work boots. His bulky red sweater, and the old Army surplus jacket he wore over it, were speckled with wood chips. Casey had no trouble at all believing he'd chopped every stick of firewood in the shed. The man looked like every woman's lumberjack fantasy.

His eyes flicked past Casey, and settled on Emma.

Typical. Guys always noticed Emma first. Casey was more than used to it. But for some reason—probably because of the harrowing drive down the mountain— tonight it bothered her more than usual.

But it wasn't the lumberjack who returned Emma's greeting. It was the other man—a bit shorter, a bit thinner, a bit less handsome, but still way above average in the good-looks department—who grinned and waved.

"Hello, ladies! Lost?"

"I don't think so," Emma said as the four of them met on the path leading to the front porch. The walk had been shoveled recently, but the new snow was quickly recoating the flagstones. "This is Dutch Gorge Lodge, isn't it?"

The men exchanged a look.

"Yeah," the shorter guy said. "It is."

"Then we're in the right place." Emma flashed him a smile, then batted her eyelashes at the lumberjack. "We have reservations for the Christmas weekend."

"Really?" Mr. Talkative asked. "Are you sure?"

"Well, of course we are! Do you think we would have driven all the way out here from Manhattan if we weren't? And I have to say," Emma continued, "the lodge is beautiful. It looks just like the picture in the brochure. So romantic! Just what we were hoping for."

Amusement flashed in the lumberjack's blue eyes.

"Well, then," the shorter man said, with an air of resignation. "Come on in, and Aunt Bea will sort everything out. I'm Jake, by the way. Jake Van der Staappen. And this is my brother, Matt."

"You two are brothers?" Emma exclaimed. "Why, we're sisters. I'm Emma. Emma Harbison. And this is Casey."

"Sisters, huh?" A sudden, wide grin blossomed on

Jake's face. He elbowed his brother. "Sisters! Well, hallelujah. I am damn happy to hear that. Aren't you, Matt?"

It was the lumberjack's turn to look resigned. He snorted and shook his head.

Casey was getting impatient with the brothers' obscure innuendo, whatever that was all about. "Um...you think we could take this conversation inside? Maybe before we freeze to death?"

"Sure thing," Jake said easily. He took Emma's arm. "Right this way, ladies."

Casey started up the flagstone path after them.

"Just watch your step," he said over his shoulder. "The walk is kinda—"

Casey's heel hit a patch of ice. "Aaaah—!"

She felt what happened next as if in slow motion. Her legs gave way; her upper body lurched backward. Her arms circled wildly, as if she could catch her balance on the frozen air. No go. She felt herself fall...

The arms that caught her were solid, strong, and warm. She blinked up, into the lumberjack's blue, blue eyes. For an instant, he held her frozen in a pose straight out of *Dancing With the Stars.*

"—kinda icy," Jake finished lamely.

And then the world turned right-side up again, and Casey's feet were once more planted firmly on the ground.

"Oh, God," Emma laughed. "I wish I'd caught that on video. Casey, you should have seen yourself. That was definitely one of your better moments."

Casey shot a dark look at Em's furry hood.

Jake quirked an eyebrow. "Your sister falls down a lot?"

"More often it's other stuff hitting the ground," Emma confided, one hand on Jake's arm. "She's terribly clumsy, poor dear. In high school, they used to call her Klutzy Casey."

Heat rushed Casey's face. She glared at Emma, sure her eyes were spitting sparks. Emma smirked and tossed her head. It was obvious her sister's snarky little comment was payback for Casey's behind-the-wheel bitchiness. Which was probably well-deserved, Casey reflected.

Not that she was going to admit it. On the contrary. She was planning to kill Emma. First chance she got.

Jake's eyes cut from one sister to the other. "Ah, well," he said hastily. "Anyone could be a klutz in this weather. There's a wicked layer of ice under all this new snow." He caught Emma below the elbow. "Here, let me help you..."

Casey watched as the pair made their way to the farmhouse porch, Jake's arm sliding around Emma's waist. She fought an urge to roll her eyes. The Todd drama wasn't even forty-eight hours old, and Emma hadn't even seriously started fishing for a replacement. And here was one already gulping down the hook.

Matt cleared his throat.

She looked up, her face going even hotter than before. She could practically feel the snow sizzling as it hit her skin.

"Think you can manage the path to the house alone?" he asked. "Or should I carry you, too?"

She nearly choked. "Not necessary." Though she was fairly certain Mr. Lumberjack was strong enough to pick her up and throw her over his shoulder. That thought brought another rush of heat.

God. What a farce this Adirondack trip was turning out to be. She couldn't wait to hole up in her room and count the hours until Christmas was over and she could leave.

Good thing she'd brought her computer.

***

"Twenty bucks, big brother." Jake's grin stretched from ear to ear. "Sisters. Not lesbians."

Matt eyed the two women standing under the flickering gaslight in the foyer, chatting with Aunt Bea. With a sigh, he extracted his wallet from his back pocket and pulled out a crisp Andrew Jackson.

"It was a logical assumption," he said as the money disappeared into his brother's pocket. "Those two look nothing alike. And this is supposed to be a couples' weekend. Exclusively. I know for a fact Aunt Bea was not expecting three couples and a pair of sisters."

Jake shrugged. "Call it a gift from the heavens. A Christmas miracle. Jesus. What an angel."

He was talking about the blonde sister, of course. Jake had a thing for blondes. This one was incredibly beautiful. Big blue eyes, high cheekbones, bright smile, unsmudged makeup. She was incredibly busty, given her size two body. Or maybe she just had an incredible plastic surgeon. She did look...plastic.

By contrast, the other sister looked...real. A bit taller, a bit heavier, a good bit less round in the chest, and no makeup as far as he could tell. She appeared much less breakable. And much less pleased with life. She had smudges under her eyes and her lips were pressed into a frown. Her dark hair was a tangled mass of curls.

"Just let me remind you," he told Jake, "we're here to work. Not to hit on the guests."

"I'll be discreet," Jake said. "Hell, I'll be anything if it gets me close to Emma. Man, oh man, does she fill out that sweater. And those legs—"

But Matt had stopped listening to his brother.

"...always wanted to act in the theater," Jake's blonde—Emma—was saying to Aunt Bea's interested nod. "On Broadway. So Casey and I, we moved to New York last spring. From Florida. That's where we grew up."

"You're a Broadway actress, dear? How lovely."

Aunt Bea glanced at Matt over her bifocals. Matt nearly groaned out loud. An aspiring actress? God Almighty, he should have known. She had the look.

"Well, not yet," Emma was saying, "but Broadway's been my dream forever! So far, though, I haven't had much luck getting into any auditions. I just don't know the right people."

"Oh, Christ." Jake made a low sound of disgust. "An actress. It just figures. If Emma finds out who you are, my chances with her are toast."

"Your chances and my sanity," Matt grumbled.

"Jesus, Matt, we gotta do something."

Matt cut him a glance. "Like what?"

"Like...I don't know, but something quick. Aunt Bea's thirty seconds from some very helpful acting advice." He frowned. "Think she'd go for bribery? We could promise to polish the good silver. Or chop another three cords of wood."

Not a bad idea, Matt thought as his aunt drew a breath to reply to Emma. Just in time, he caught Bea's gaze, and made a cutting motion with his hand.

No, he mouthed. Don't tell her...

Aunt Bea pursed her lips and turned her attention back to Emma. "Acting is such a challenging career, dear. It's hard to get started. It does help to know the right people." She gave Matt a speaking glance. "Or so I've been told by...people...who know the business."

Jake groaned. "That's it. She's gonna spill, and I'm gonna officially drop off the face of the planet as far as Emma's concerned. Though I suppose I might have a shot at the klutzy sister..."

"No." Matt was not in the mood to spend the next four days dodging the attentions of a wannabe actress. He reached the desk in two strides.

"Aunt Bea?" He slid a hand under her elbow. "Can I talk to you a moment?"

"Matthew! I was just about to tell Emma about your—"

"*Now*, Aunt Bea. Jake can take over the check-in."

A smiling Jake quickly stepped up to the antique roll-top desk where Aunt Bea kept her reservations ledger. "It would be my pleasure, ladies."

Bea frowned as Matt guided her to the alcove under the stair. He lowered his voice. "Aunt Bea. Don't tell that woman anything. Please."

"But Matthew, why not? Emma's an aspiring actress, new to the city, and you're always looking for new talent."

"True enough, but I just don't want to get into it this weekend. I came upstate to help you and Uncle Fred, not to add to my call list. Just keep quiet about the agency, okay?"

Bea was not pleased. "Emma's a guest, Matthew. And she seems like such a nice girl—"

"I'll have Jake get her number." Matt was getting truly desperate, to agree to that. He was one of the most sought after casting directors in the city—only one starry-eyed newbie actress in a hundred made his Broadway call list. Though he could probably swing Emma a TV commercial if she wasn't completely hopeless. She had the looks for it, anyway.

"I'll call her in for an interview and screen test after the holidays," he said. "But only if you promise not to say anything to her while she's here. And that goes for Uncle Fred, too."

The twin lines between his aunt's eyes deepened. "Well, all right, Matthew, if you insist. But I really don't underst—"

"Why are these sisters here, anyway? I thought only couples were booked for the Romance of Christmas weekend."

"Yes, well, that's true. But apparently Emma and her

boyfriend stopped dating just a few days ago, poor dear. So she brought her sister with her instead."

Ah. So that explained why the wild-haired sister looked less than thrilled. She hadn't wanted to come. Dutch Gorge in December wasn't everyone's idea of a vacation, least of all, Matt supposed, someone from Florida.

He guided Bea back to the sisters. His brother's head was bent over the reservation ledger.

"You ladies are in the Daisy room," Jake said.

"That's our nicest room," Aunt Bea said. "Almost a suite. It's a bit of a climb, of course, up to the third floor. But it does have a private bath."

"It sounds perfect," Emma said.

"Jake," Matt interjected, "why don't you take Emma to her room? Her sister can show me what luggage to bring up."

"Right," Jake said, springing into action. "Emma, right this way. Here, let me take your coat. Casey, careful out there on the path." He winked. "Wouldn't want Matt here to throw his back out..."

Emma laughed. Casey shot a glare at her sister, before turning to follow Matt back out to the porch. Full night had fallen. The muted light shining through the bay window cast a warm glow into the dark. Even in the yellow gaslight, Casey looked pale. And tired.

"Long drive up from the city?"

She snorted. "Only about five hours too long. And then it started snowing, and we missed the turn into the gorge, and the road got slippery, and we got into a fight... God. I can't believe I let my sister talk me into coming out here."

"Ah well, at least you made it safely."

"Barely. Who built that road, anyway? We're lucky we didn't go over the side of the freaking mountain! I'm telling you, if we survive the drive home, I am going to kill that woman. Slowly."

Her voice was trembling. More from fear than from true anger, Matt thought. A delayed reaction to a drive that had truly frightened her.

"The road into the gorge can be dicey," he said. "Especially in a snowfall. First northern winter, I take it?"

She shivered. "Yes."

"Driving on snow takes a bit of practice. But don't worry. You'll get used to it."

She made a sound of disdain. "I'd rather not, thank you."

Man, but she was prickly. With that frown and all that crazy hair, she looked like a disgruntled hedgehog. But even so...he scrutinized her more closely. Now that she wasn't standing next to her stunning sister, he realized she wasn't as plain as he'd first thought. She had the kind of look he'd have cast for a best-friend role. A pleasant face, with good bone structure. He thought her eyes were brown. Maybe. It was hard to tell in the dark. She was probably even pretty when she smiled.

She wasn't smiling at the moment. She looked ready to strangle someone. Her sister, most likely. He swallowed a laugh.

Production title: Sidekick. Woman perpetually trapped in her sister's misadventures finally snaps, revealing a dangerous violent streak...

He shook the thought out of his head. Christ. Hadn't he just told Aunt Bea he didn't want to think about work? Unfortunately, the drive upstate hadn't put the brakes on his obsessive habit of casting everyone around him into imaginary dramas.

The snow was coming down in a thick curtain now, the steady north wind whistling down the gorge. A rogue gust picked up a swirl of new-fallen snow off the front yard and threw it into their faces.

Casey gripped the lapels of her coat, savagely wrenching the fabric tight across her chest. Not that it was going to do her any good. The flimsy thing was designed for a city winter. Not a mountain one.

"God, it's cold." Her teeth were actually chattering.

"Actually, it's barely below twenty," Matt said, purely for the enjoyment of seeing her scowl deepen. "But it's supposed to drop to single digits tonight."

"Lovely," she muttered.

He took pity on her. "Listen, if you're that cold, just give me your key and tell me how many bags you've got. No need to come with me to your car."

"No." She hugged the coat tighter. "You won't be able to carry it all by yourself. Emma is not a light packer."

She stepped off the porch, tripped on the first step, and lunged down the rest. He barely managed to catch hold of her arm before she landed face-first in the snow.

"Wow. Your sister wasn't kidding, was she? About you making a habit of falling?"

She jerked her sleeve out of his grip. "I'm fine. It's just these boots. They're not the best on ice."

Matt extracted a small flashlight from his pocket. "Here. This might help."

"Thanks."

She plowed through the snow, following the thin beam of light, placing each step with care. "Damn it's dark out here," she said. "And quiet."

"That's the snow. It muffles everything."

They managed to reach her car without further mishap. "Nice park job," he commented.

"Bite your tongue."

He chuckled. "Another inch and Jake's bumper would have turned your fender into crumpled aluminum foil."

"I know." She climbed over the snow bank to open the trunk. The interior revealed a pair of pink suitcases and a worn navy blue duffle.

Matt handed Casey the flashlight and started collecting the bags, slinging the duffle over his shoulder and hefting the suitcases. Christ. The bigger pink one must be filled with bricks. He didn't have to ask who it belonged to.

"Your sister planning to stay the month?"

"Emma likes to be prepared." Casey reached into the trunk for one last bag.

"Might as well leave that one," he told her.

She glanced up at him. "What?"

"That's a computer, right?"

"Yes."

"Then why bring it in? You won't be able to use it."

She straightened, setting one hand on the open trunk door and trying to grip both her bag and his flashlight in the other. The beam bounced wildly.

"You mean because this God-forsaken crack in the Earth's crust is in a satellite blind spot? I already know that. My GPS lost its signal even before we started down the mountain. So I'm guessing there'll be no Internet, either. But that's okay. I can work offline."

He snorted. "Can you work without electricity?"

She froze in the act of slamming the trunk. Her eyes jerked to his, and even in the darkness, he could tell they were appalled.

"Without...*electricity?* You can't be serious."

"Perfectly serious, honey. Dutch Lodge is off the grid."

Her head swiveled toward the house. "But...there are lights—"

"Gas light," he said. "And oil lamps. Don't tell me you didn't notice? It's usually the first thing that guests comment on."

"No." Her voice was barely more than a whisper. "I didn't notice. But...what about TV? Hot water?" She sucked in a breath. *"Heat?"*

"Sorry, no TV. But there's plenty of hot water, courtesy of a mountain spring Uncle Fred piped in years ago. A large propane tank out back takes care of the gaslights and water heaters. And there's a fireplace or wood burning stove in every room. Don't worry, you'll get your hot baths, and you won't freeze."

"But—no electricity? How can anyone live without electricity?"

He laughed. "It's not so bad. I grew up here, you know, and managed to survive."

"But...but..."

The sounds of her sputtering shock made him wish for a stronger flashlight. "You really didn't know about the electricity? It's all in the brochure your sister was waving arou—" He cut off, and laughed outright.

"What's so funny?" she demanded.

"You didn't read that brochure, did you? And your sister didn't tell you."

Casey slammed the trunk. The crash echoed off the sides of the gorge like a gunshot.

"No," she ground out between clenched teeth. "I didn't and she didn't. But she is certainly going to answer for it now."

Still clutching her laptop case, she flung herself in the direction of the house, her footsteps hard and fast. Well, as hard and fast as footsteps could get in six inches of new snow.

"You know," he said, juggling the baggage as he fell into step beside her. "Most guests at Dutch Lodge consider the lack of electricity a good thing. In fact, it's the reason most people come here. To get away from civilization."

"Yes, well, I like civilization just fine. I don't want to get away from it. No electricity," she added under her breath. "This is insane. That brat is going to die. Painfully."

That repressed violent streak again, Matt thought, impressed.

"She's just lucky I've got some battery life. If I make it to tomorrow morning, I might let her live."

"Why?" Matt asked. "What happens tomorrow morning?"

She spun toward him, stumbling, then catching her balance. The flashlight beam glanced off the white ground. "What happens tomorrow morning is that we're leaving. Whether Emma wants to or not."

Matt couldn't suppress another bark of laughter. "Leaving? Sorry to disappoint, but I really doubt that's gonna happen."

"Oh, it's going to happen, all right. The instant the sun comes up, I'm outta here."

The wind chose just that moment to kick up a wintery blast. "I'm curious," Matt shouted over the rising gale. "Did you happen to check the local weather report before plunging into the gorge?"

They'd reached the house. Casey stomped up the three steps to the porch before turning to glare down at him. "No."

He grinned.

Trepidation crept into her voice. "Why do you ask?"

"Because I was listening to the update on the shortwave just before you got here. This storm's turning nasty, and it's going to last all night. They're predicting two feet."

"Two feet?" Her mouth fell open. "Of *snow?*"

"Well, not of rose petals," he said. "So I'm pretty sure no one's going anywhere tomorrow. Least of all you."

Chapter Three

The farmhouse living room was cozy and welcoming, with flames snapping cheerfully in a fireplace hung with Christmas stockings and decorated with fresh-cut holly. A brass gaslight chandelier supplied a general glow of romantic illumination, while glass-topped oil lanterns filled in the corners. Casey couldn't believe she hadn't noticed the lack of light bulbs on her first trip into the house.

The non-electric illumination was, she supposed, enchanting. Muted, and a little mysterious. Though it did mean that the Christmas tree, decorated with intricate blown-glass ornaments, wasn't lit up like...well, like a Christmas tree.

An elaborate Nativity scene, complete with angels, shepherds, and kings, was arranged on a low table nestled close to the evergreen boughs. As for the rest of the room, it was a cozy collection of furnishings—some antique, others just old. The walls were hung with oil paintings of nature scenes, except for one large watercolor of a windmill. A spinet piano, its cherry finish polished to a deep luster, stood against one wall.

A low buzz of happy chatter circulated in the cinnamon-scented air. Casey's gaze flicked over a half dozen lodge guests, separated into three happy pairs. One couple snuggled in a gold plush loveseat, while another stood at the big bay window, arms entwined, watching the snow fall. Couple Number Three stood in front of the Christmas tree, exclaiming in low tones over the antique ornaments.

And then there was Couple Number Four. Emma and Jake. Casey's sister nestled in an overstuffed armchair near the fire, sipping a mug of something steaming. Jake sat on the chair's arm, one arm across its padded back, talking in animated tones. Even though there was a perfectly empty armchair two feet to his left.

Casey adjusted her grip on her laptop case handle and stalked toward them.

Neither noticed her beeline approach. Jake gestured with his free hand, touching Emma's shoulder. Emma laughed, her low, throaty chuckle prompting Jake to lean even closer. He darted a subtle glance at Emma's cleavage. If the man was a dog, Casey thought uncharitably, drool would be dripping from his open mouth.

She stepped into her sister's line of vision. "We need to talk, Emma. Now."

Emma smiled up at her, but the expression was belied by the frost in her eye. She was still angry.

But Emma was an actress, and right now, Jake was her audience. She smiled sweetly. "Casey! Isn't this room cozy? The tree is so beautiful. And the fire is delicious."

The heat on Casey's back did feel good. Especially after that frigid trek to the car and back. But she was damned if she was going to admit it. "That's neither here nor there," she said. "You've got some explaining—"

Jake jumped to his feet. "Um... Would you like something hot to drink, Casey? Tea? Spiced cider? Hot chocolate?"

"Oh, let Jake get you some of the spiced cider," Emma said. "It's very good."

"Fine," Casey snapped. Anything to get rid of Emma's adoring puppy.

"Coming right up," Jake said.

***

Jake headed Matt off at the bottom of the stairs.

"I need a favor," he said.

"What, after taking my twenty dollars? You gotta be kidding."

"I'm dead serious. That Emma is a wet dream come true. And she just dumped some loser of a boyfriend. Which makes the timing even better. Rebound sex is the best."

Matt lowered Emma's rock-filled pink suitcase to the floor. "So? Have at it. What's stopping you?"

"Her sister. The woman is out of her mind. She's not a happy camper."

"That's because Emma didn't tell her about the electricity," Matt said. "You should have seen Casey's face when I told her."

Her expression had been priceless. If she'd have

walked into Matt's agency, he'd have immediately cast her into a TV commercial—maybe one for laundry detergent. As the housewife who discovers a pack of muddy dogs mauling her newly washed basket of whites.

But Casey wasn't looking to be cast in a TV commercial. Or a print campaign, or a theater production. She wasn't an actress. She wasn't drop-dead gorgeous. She was just a normal woman. Matt chuckled. A normal woman with a hidden violent streak.

"Whatever," Jake said impatiently. "The thing is, she's getting Emma all uptight. The two of them are spitting like cats. Do you think you could distract Casey a bit tonight? You know, so Emma and I can have a little time alone? Please? A few private hours with that woman would really brighten up this drudge week for me."

Matt and Jake had been helping out with Dutch Lodge's Christmas weekend for five years now, so the middle-aged married couple their aunt and uncle employed could spend Christmas with their married daughter in Montreal. Jake came solely out of a sense of duty—he'd much rather spend Christmas in Boston. Matt, on the other hand, looked forward to the trip each year. To him, five days of mindless manual labor—chopping wood, shoveling snow, cooking and serving meals—was a perfect antidote to the pressures of his city life. God knew just the thought of spending a few days out of touch by email and cell was heaven.

"Come on, Matt. Will you do it?" Jake said. "Keep Casey out of Emma's hair?"

And here was another chore Matt really didn't mind.

"Tell you what," he said, handing off the pink suitcases to Jake. "Haul Emma's bags of rocks up to the third floor, and I'll distract Casey for as long as you want."

***

"Isn't he cute?" Emma said, her eyes on Jake as he left the room. "And he really seems to like me."

"Big deal." Casey sank into the empty armchair opposite her sister. She put her computer case on the floor between her feet. "Every man likes you."

"Jake's brother doesn't."

"That's ridiculous."

"No, it's not. He's barely made eye contact with me. Every time I look at him, he grimaces and looks away."

"I really doubt that," Casey said. "But it hardly matters. Emma, this place doesn't have electricity! Why didn't you tell me?"

Emma's eyes slid away. "Because you never would have come if you'd known."

"Damn right, I wouldn't have come! I have a New Year's Eve deadline! I need to work. And now there's a freaking blizzard. We could be stuck here for days without so much as a single electrical outlet. I can't believe you'd do this to me."

"Well, I can't believe you can't handle a few days away from that damn computer. Especially on Christmas, for chrissakes. Casey, you work sixty hours a week as it is! Do you have to work on Christmas, too?"

"Someone has to pay our rent. Waitressing doesn't pay

squat."

Emma's eyes turned frigid, and her next words dripped ice. "That was low, Case. And don't think I've forgiven you for what you said in the car. You can be such a bitch sometimes."

"The truth hurts, doesn't it?" Casey muttered, then immediately wished the words back when real hurt flared in Emma's eyes.

"You have no room to criticize me. Just look at yourself. All you do is work, and surf the Internet, and play computer games. We've been in New York for nine months, and you haven't even tried to make a single real friend. Every time I invite you to a party, you turn me down."

Heat crept up Casey's neck. She tried to tell herself it was because of the fireplace. "I went to some of your parties. I can't stand the type of people you're trying so hard to impress." *And I can't stand how dull I feel next to them.* "Actors. Models. Agents. Producers. There's not a single genuine person in a hundred of them."

"Well," a masculine voice said. "On that note, here you go." A solid set of jeans-clad legs and a steaming mug appeared in front of Casey.

She looked up into a pair of dark blue eyes. Not Jake. Matt. He quirked a brow at her. Just great. He'd heard her whole rant. And now he probably thought she was a bitch. No—worse. A clumsy bitch.

"Um...thanks." She accepted her mug, sipping to cover her embarrassment.

"Where's Jake?" Emma asked.

"Taking your bags to your room," Matt said without looking over at her. "And after that we're both due in the kitchen. So if you ladies will excuse me...? "

"Of course," Emma said.

Casey let out a long breath as he moved away.

"Way to go, Case," Emma said. "Let every man within a hundred miles know how stuck up you are." She turned to stare into the fire, sipping her cider.

Casey placed her own mug on the table next to her chair. Emma was right. Casey's temper and sharp tongue—not to mention her insecurities—tended to get her in trouble. Almost as often as her clumsiness produced bruises. Emma, on the other hand, was grace and graciousness personified. Not for the first time, Casey wondered if one of them had been switched at birth. It certainly would explain some things.

She zipped open her case and powered up her laptop. Just as she expected: her satellite Internet account status icon had a big fat red "X" over it. No service.

Mrs. Van der Staappen—or Aunt Bea, as she insisted everyone call her, called her guests to dinner a few minutes later. Matt's aunt was a plump, pleasant woman with short gray hair and a ruffled apron. Her husband, Uncle Fred, sported a grizzled white beard trimmed in Dutch style, with no mustache. He looked like a friendly old lion in plaid shirt and suspenders.

The meal was served family style, and was already laid out on the long farmhouse table when Casey and Emma entered the dining room. Aunt Bea and Uncle Fred took places at either end, while their eight guests and two nephews filled in the chairs on either side. Emma smiled as Jake slid into the empty seat beside her. Casey studied her flatware as Matt, coming in late from the kitchen, dropped into the only available seat, on Casey's left.

The fare was hearty and simple: pot roast, peas, and mashed potatoes, with apple pie for dessert. The dinner conversation centered, of course, on the weather. The storm was a blowing with a vengeance now, whistling and rattling the window panes.

"Been a while since we had a good blizzard," Uncle Fred commented over coffee.

Privately, Casey didn't think the words "good" and "blizzard" belonged in the same sentence.

"Especially this early in the season," Fred continued. "It's shaping up to be a doozie. But don't you folks worry none—we're snug as bugs here in the valley."

"Will the road out of the gorge be cleared tomorrow?" Casey ventured.

"Oh, no, honey," Aunt Bea said with a soft laugh. "I imagine it will take at least two days for the county snow plows to get to us. Maybe even three."

Tomorrow was Christmas Eve. So in other words, Casey was stuck here until at least the day after Christmas.

Matt gave her a subtle elbow in the ribs. Her head whipped around in time to see his lips quirk. Casey could almost hear him thinking *I told you so.*

"Oh, it sounds so romantic," one of the female guests

sighed. She leaned into her husband. "Max and I have never been snowbound before."

"Me neither," Emma said, her eyes dancing. "It's going to be so much fun. Casey and I just moved to New York from Florida, you know. We've never so much as packed a single snowball before."

"Looks like I'll have a lot to teach you this weekend." Jake's seductive whisper, aimed for Emma, was loud enough for Casey—and Matt—to overhear.

Emma giggled.

Casey scowled.

Matt just chuckled.

Chapter Four

Casey was still camped out in the dining room.

Matt ducked back in the kitchen, wiping his hands on a dishtowel. He'd been keeping an eye on her all evening, but so far he hadn't needed to haul her away from her sister. Just the opposite. Right after dessert was cleared, Casey had powered up her laptop at the dining room table. She'd ignored Emma all night. Matt was pretty sure Emma hadn't even noticed. She was too wrapped up with Jake.

Matt had washed and dried the dinner dishes, and prepped the kitchen for tomorrow's breakfast. All with minimal help from Jake, who'd disappeared with Emma more than an hour ago, right after Aunt Bea and Uncle Fred had finished delivering firewood and complimentary champagne to the guest rooms.

His work done, Matt propped one shoulder on the door jamb between the kitchen and dining room, eyeing Dutch Lodge's most reluctant guest. It was well after eleven, and everyone else had gone to sleep—or at least, he amended, to bed.

But Casey was still tapping away at her computer, her wild curls sprouting from her scalp in every direction.

Every few seconds, she'd drag a hand through the mop, making it worse.

Production: TV Commercial. Product: Curl control hair gel. Harried career woman rushes through a typical day, losing precious minutes every time she pauses to tame her wild hair. Finally, a concerned friend offers to share her new hair gel...

Matt shook himself out of his reverie. He wasn't quite sure why he found Casey so fascinating. She certainly had a sharp tongue. And she seemed much more interested in her laptop than in any flesh-and-blood people.

What kind of work was so important she had to do it on Christmas vacation, anyway? He shoved off the door jamb and peered over her shoulder at the screen.

She was playing that candy smashing game everyone was addicted to. He laughed. "I thought you had work do."

She blasted a row of lemon drops without looking up. "I do. But I'm too pissed at my sister to concentrate on it."

"What is it that you do? For a job, I mean."

"I'm a computer programmer. I work for an interactive agency."

"What's that, exactly?"

"We do viral marketing via mobile communications and social networking. Like, for example, the project I'm working on is a contest sponsored by Diva Diamonds. You know, the big jewelry chain?" He nodded as a gumdrop exploded. "Well, starting at nine on New Year's Eve, contestants can upload pictures of the perfect romantic kiss via three social media sites. The photos will scroll on the Diva Diamonds website, and simultaneously on a billboard in Times Square. From nine until midnight, anyone can upvote or downvote the entries with a text message. The top voted kiss will appear in Times Square at midnight, and the couple in it will win a Diva Diamonds tiara and a trip to Paris."

"Wow. Interesting."

"Ha. A pain in the butt, is what it's been."

She pulverized another row of sweets. He leaned forward just a little, his chest bumping the back of her head.

"Damn. Do you mind? You're crowding me."

He moved back a step. "So how much juice you got left in that thing?" he said after a few minutes.

"Probably not much." She clicked the battery icon and grimaced. "In fact, hardly any at all."

She played a minute or so longer, then sighed when the low battery warning came on. Powering down the computer, she stowed it back in its case.

"Shoulda paced yourself," he commented. "You have at least two more days here."

She sat back in her chair, glancing up at him, and then away. "I know. I'll be bored out of my skull tomorrow. I'll probably be reduced to reading Emma's fashion magazines. By the way, have you seen her?"

"Not in a while." He crossed the room and glanced into the living room. "I'm pretty sure everyone's gone up to their rooms. The Romance of Christmas and all. You and I are the only ones left down here."

"Right." She stood, hefting the computer case in one hand. "Well, I guess I'll go up, too. Emma's probably waiting for me."

Matt doubted that. He knew his brother only too well.

"Good night, then," Casey said.

He suppressed a grin. "Um...watch yourself going up the stairs. The gaslights are on the lowest setting."

He followed her into the foyer, then stood at the bottom of the stairs as her footsteps faded toward the third floor. The far-away rattle of a doorknob ensued. Then muted pounding. Then muffled voices.

Matt leaned against the newel post, waiting through the brief silence that followed. The footsteps returned, descending, heavier and angrier than they'd been on the way up. He gave in to a laugh.

Casey stomped down the last six steps from the landing, computer case in one hand, blue duffle in the other, her dark eyes flashing fire. With her wild curls sticking out from her head in every direction, she looked like Medusa.

"Something wrong?" he asked innocently.

"Yes, something's wrong. My sister locked me out and left my bag in the hall. I need another room." Her eyes narrowed. "You knew it, too, didn't you?"

"I had my suspicions," Matt said. "I saw Emma leading my impressionable little brother up the stairs about an hour ago."

"Impressionable? Jake? Oh, please—"

"And I might've gone up to the third floor a little while

after that, and noticed your duffle outside your door."

She huffed. "You could have warned me."

"What, and miss out on the chance for a bit of entertainment? It's boring out here in the country. You have to take whatever amusement you can get."

"Yeah, well, you can stop being amused and find me another room. Emma's not going to open that door before morning."

His smile faded. "Are you sure she won't let up in an hour or so? I can't believe your sister would lock you out all night."

"Believe it. She's really pissed at me." She sighed. "It's partly my own fault, I suppose. First we fought in the car, then I was so angry when I found out about the electricity. I said a few nasty things to her. This is her way of getting back at me."

"You and your sister fight a lot?"

"Like cats and dogs," Casey admitted. "We always have. But it never lasts. Believe it or not, we're actually very close. Emma will be all smiles by morning. But until then...just point me toward an empty room and I'll get out of your hair."

"Well," Matt said. "That's going to be a problem. Because there isn't one."

"It doesn't have to be anything fancy. I don't need a private bath—"

"Didn't you hear me? This isn't a huge house, and it's full. There is no empty bedroom. Bath or no bath."

Casey blinked. Then she sat down abruptly, on the

second-to-last stair. "You're kidding me."

"No. Sorry. I'm not."

"Then where am I supposed to sleep? On one of the loveseats in the living room?"

"Wouldn't be my choice." Matt paused. "Want me to go up and drag my brother's ass out of your room? I can do it easily enough. I outweigh him by twenty pounds, and I've got a master key."

"No," Casey shook her head, setting her curls dancing. "No way. You don't want to interrupt what's going on in there, believe me. Emma doesn't believe in slow courtship."

Matt laughed. "Neither does Jake."

"And I wouldn't want to brave Emma's wrath if you do throw Jake out." She sighed. "I guess it's a loveseat for me. Or maybe one of those big armchairs by the fireplace. They were pretty comfortable."

He hesitated. "Or...you could sleep where Jake was supposed to."

She blinked up at him through inky black eyelashes. "And where might that be?"

"With me."

***

I cannot believe I agreed to sleep with this guy.

Or, more accurately, sleep in his room.

Talk about embarrassing! But Casey hardly had a choice. There was no way she was going to confront Emma before morning. It would only lead to a shouting match. They'd wake up everyone in the lodge.

"This way," Matt said, leading the way, her duffle slung

over one broad shoulder.

She clutched her dead computer and trailed after him, blinking when he stopped at the closet to get their coats. "Here," he said, handing her hers. "You'll need this."

She took it. "What for?"

"I don't sleep in the farmhouse," he said. "I stay in a cabin out back, in the woods behind the barn."

A cabin in the woods. Well, that was good, wasn't it? A cabin had to be bigger than a regular bedroom. It probably had multiple rooms. She followed Matt through the kitchen, where the massive iron woodstove supplied a lingering warmth, and the scent of baked apples still hung in the air. A small mudroom led to the back door. Matt opened it on a blast of wind and snow. The world beyond was white.

"Oh, my God."

Matt gripped her upper arm and pulled her into the blizzard, slamming the door behind him. She hoped he knew where he was heading, because his flashlight barely made a dent in the night. But his stride was quick and sure. The wind abruptly died as they rounded the side of the barn and slipped into the bare winter wood. A minute later, she stumbled up two steps to a small porch. She huddled under the shelter of a meager overhang while he shoved open the door.

God. She was frozen, and it wasn't much warmer inside the cabin than out. She rubbed her mitten-clad hands and stomped the snow off her boots while Matt struck a match. He lit the oil lantern standing on a small table by the door.

The room jumped to life. The single room. Which wasn't, she noted with some trepidation, all that much bigger than a bedroom.

The walls were rough logs, unadorned except for the deer head mounted over a small stone fireplace. Ugh. She could almost feel its glassy eyes staring. There was a kitchenette of sorts, consisting of two feet of counter, an old-fashioned ice-box, and a small wood stove. A few dirty dishes were stacked in a soapstone sink.

Furnishings were few and simple. A tall wardrobe, an unmade double bed. A droopy leather couch faced the hearth, and the big square table sat in the center of the room under an oil lamp chandelier. The underside of the ceiling above was black with soot.

She wandered to a bookshelf crowded with animal skulls, birds' nests, rocks, trinkets, and, yes, even a few dusty novels. Out of the jumble, one item caught her eye. A wooden cube, fashioned from at least five different kinds of wood joined with flawless precision. The workmanship was beautiful.

"Try to open it."

She started, surprised to find Matt standing behind her.

"It's a box?" she asked, intrigued.

"Yeah." His blue eyes smiled down at her, and for a second, she forgot to breathe. "Go on. See if you can figure it out."

She ignored the funny jump in her stomach. And the

way her skin suddenly seemed to be tingling all over. Concentrating on the box, she turned it over in her hands. There didn't seem to be a latch. Or any hinges. She ran her thumbs along the sides, trying to slide one of the panels. Nothing.

"You're not kidding me? This thing really opens?"

"Yes. It's a mystery box." The corners of his eyes crinkled. "Don't tell me a smart girl like you is giving up so quickly."

"Maybe not so smart after all," she mumbled.

He chuckled. "To open it...you have to press just...here." He touched one corner. "Then slide this side up, then twist here..."

She followed the complicated instructions. At the end of the sequence, one side of the box popped open. The compartment inside was empty.

"No mysteries revealed," she said.

"I guess the mystery is how I ever had the patience to make the thing in the first place," Matt said with a laugh.

She followed the sequence in reverse, marveling as the panels slid back into place. "You really made this?"

"When I was fifteen. Took an entire winter. But I had a lot of time on my hands back then."

"I guess so," she said, placing the box carefully back on the shelf. "You had no TV, no stereo, no video games...I can't even imagine it."

"It's a wonder I survived, huh?"

"You still live here," Casey pointed out. "So it must be possible."

He hesitated. "I don't, actually."

"Don't what?"

"Live here. I left the gorge when I turned eighteen. I only come for visits now. Mostly in the summer, when there's more activity. My aunt and uncle run a campground from spring to fall, you know."

"No, I didn't know."

"It's all in the brochure."

"That would be the brochure I didn't read, remember?"

He set her duffle on a bench under the window. She stowed her computer on the floor beside it.

"Jake's been sleeping on the couch," he said. "But you can take my bed if you want." Amusement flashed in his eyes. "Aunt Bea likes her guests to be comfortable."

Sleep in his bed? The tangle of blankets and pillows on the couch looked a whole lot safer. "Um...no. I wouldn't want to put you out. Thanks. The couch is fine. It'll be warmer near the fire, anyway."

"True enough." Matt crossed to the hearth and began building up the fire, throwing on two logs from an iron basket. He jabbed at them with a poker. Sparks and flames leapt.

"I don't snore, by the way," he added, glancing back at her. "How 'bout you?"

He sounded like he might be teasing, but she couldn't be sure. "I don't think so." A sudden, panicked thought struck. "Please tell me there's a bathroom in this cabin."

"Over there." Matt jerked his chin at a narrow door half-hidden by the wardrobe.

"Oh, thank God."

Finished with the fire, he placed his hands on his thighs and rose. Casey was struck again by how tall he was. And broad. If he stretched his arm up, he could easily touch the bottom of the cabin's rafters. But it was his face that really made her nervous. It was just so...perfect. He'd fit right in with Emma's collection of beautiful acting friends.

"You can come over here by the fire," he said. "And take your coat off. I promise not to bite."

With some reluctance, she made her way to his side. The intimacy of this small cabin was disconcerting. She stared into the leaping flames, all too aware of his eyes on her.

"I think I'll keep my coat on for a while," she said. "It's not that warm in here yet."

"Not used to the cold, I take it?"

"No. Sometimes I can't believe I let Emma talk me into moving north. But she has this crazy idea she's going to land a role in a Broadway production."

"But you don't think so."

"Seriously? I doubt she'll even get close. Don't get me wrong, Emma's a great actress, but Broadway? There's just so much competition. It's nuts."

"But you moved across the country anyway? Just to hold your sister's hand?"

"When Emma gets one of her big ideas, no force on Earth can talk her out of it. She was moving to New York, come hell or high water. I couldn't let her go alone."

"Why not?"

She held out her hands to the fire. Her fingers were finally starting to thaw. "Because Emma and I...we're all the family we have. She's so young, and didn't know a soul in the city... I would've worried too much if she'd come to Manhattan alone. It was no big deal for me to move, really. A computer programmer can find work anywhere."

Heat was radiating from the fire in waves now, and she was starting to sweat inside her coat. She eased open the buttons, then reluctantly retreated from the warmth of the fire to unzip her duffel.

"Um, listen, don't feel like you have to entertain me. I'm beat from the long drive. I'm just going to listen to my iPod for a while."

"Until the battery runs out?"

"Yeah. And that bathroom—?"

He made a sweeping gesture. "All yours."

She rummaged through her bag and pulled out her toiletries, along with the grey sweatpants and oversized tee-shirt she slept in. She added a sweatshirt, too, for good measure—that fire wasn't going to last all night.

The bathroom was, as Matt had warned, tiny. Basic masculine accoutrements—toothbrush, razor, comb— occupied a miniscule shelf. There was a sink with running water, and the smallest stall shower she'd ever seen. The toilet was some kind of environmental kind that didn't flush, but was otherwise surprisingly normal.

Her elbows banged against the walls as she dressed for bed. She frowned at her reflection in the mirror, appalled at the sorry state of her hair. The dry, cold air didn't do her any favors—it looked like she'd stuck her finger in an electric socket. Brushing only made things worse. With a sigh, she pushed open the door.

And stopped dead.

In her absence, Matt had also readied for bed. But the man's tolerance for sleeping in the cold was, apparently, much, much greater than Casey's.

She sucked in a breath. He lay on top of his rumpled bed, turning the pages of one of his dusty novels by the light of the lantern. The only thing covering him was a pair of boxer shorts. Absorbed in his book, he didn't so much as look up when she emerged from the bathroom. Which was a good thing, because she couldn't stop staring.

He looked like a god.

While she looked like a witch.

She grabbed her earbuds and phone, dove under her blankets, and shut her eyes.

Too late.

The image of Matt's near-naked body was burned permanently onto the insides of her eyelids.

***

It was one of his favorite Agatha Christies, and any other time, Matt would've welcomed a few quiet hours to revisit the story. But right now he simply turned the pages, without reading a single word, all his attention given to his peripheral vision. Casey was a quirky, prickly woman. She put him in mind of a porcupine. Especially with that hair. She was sarcastic and funny, but he suspected there was a vulnerable spot somewhere behind the façade. One she was trying her best to hide.

Definitely not the kind of woman he dealt with at the office. Models and actresses were a breed unto themselves. A woman didn't succeed in the business without equal amounts of bravado, style, and ruthlessness. Matt could spot the type a mile away. Casey's sister had the attitude. In spades.

He imagined Jake worshipping at Emma's altar right this very moment...and had to adjust the covers over his burgeoning erection. But not because he wanted to take his brother's place with beautiful Emma. Not by a long shot. Oddly, it was prickly, wild-haired Casey fueling his fantasy.

Matt was missing an important industry holiday party in the city tonight. Rich food, beautiful people, free-flowing booze, more BS than you could shovel with a backhoe. If he'd been there, chances were he wouldn't have left alone. There was always some woman offering to warm his bed.

His reputation as one of New York's premier casting directors had soared in the last few years. His company had handled casting for countless TV commercials, print ad campaigns, and a good number of theater productions—four on Broadway in the past year alone. He'd even, just for fun, cast an indie movie. The money had been a pittance, but the film had done well at Sundance, and the success had only added to his cachet. In short, he was in demand. Both professionally and socially.

Easy sex was part of the bargain. He'd be lying if said it hadn't been fun at first. But after a while he'd begun to notice that the less effort it took to get a woman into bed, the more dissatisfied he was the next morning. He was all too well aware that his bed partners were hoping their association with him would launch their careers to the next level. None of them cared about him as a man.

But the woman currently sacked out on his couch? She wasn't trying to land a spot in a magazine or on the stage. She didn't live from casting call to casting call. She was a normal woman, with a normal job, living a normal life.

And she'd walked right past his bed.

He glanced over the top of his book. Casey's eyes were closed, her breathing was deep and easy. White earbud wires snaked from her ears, disappearing under the covers. She'd fallen asleep with a slight scowl on her face.

She wasn't interested.

Perversely, that made him happy.

It also made him want her.

He almost laughed aloud at the absurdity of it all. Call it idiocy. Call it an experiment. But all he could think of was trying to change her mind.

Chapter Five

Casey woke to the aroma of frying bacon and perking coffee.

All in all, it wasn't a bad start to Christmas Eve morning. Her stomach recognized its good fortune a half-second before her brain did, and let out a monster growl.

Mortified, she sat up. Matt stood in the cabin's kitchenette—fully dressed, thank God—tending an iron skillet. He wore plaid flannel and blue denim, and could have easily graced the cover of a sportsmen magazine. Casey had never had a thing for the outdoorsy look. Until just this very minute.

He glanced over at her. "Hungry?"

A hot flush rose up her neck and into her cheeks. She started to drag a hand through her hair, then stopped. She'd looked like a witch last night. How much worse did she look this morning?

"You're...making breakfast?" Inane, but it was the first thing she could think of to say.

"Bacon and eggs. Do you always sleep like the dead? You didn't so much as twitch when I banged this pan on the stove."

"Yes, well, I was exhausted." She fumbled around in the blankets for her earbuds and phone. She thumbed the button. Dead. Of course. She tossed the useless thing in the general direction of her duffel.

She rose, groaning a little when her muscles protested. The couch cushions sagged in all the wrong places. She felt indescribably ratty. Her teeth were fuzzy. She wouldn't be surprised if Matt could smell her morning breath over the bacon and coffee. Grabbing some clean jeans and a top, she fled into the bathroom.

She managed a quick shower under a low-pressure flow of not-all-that-hot water. She slicked some gel on her wet hair, and wished she'd packed some makeup. Which was ridiculous. As if some eye shadow and blush was going to transform her into someone like Emma.

She emerged from the bathroom, feeling more awkward than ever. Crescents of snow rested on the outside of the window panes. Frost painted the inside of the glass.

"Is the storm over?"

"Just about." Matt transferred several slices of bacon to a plate. "A few flurries now, that's all."

"Was it as bad as they predicted?"

"Hoping to escape the gorge, are you? Sorry, but not today. Or tomorrow. We got more than expected. I measured it at thirty-three, thirty-four inches."

She felt a spike of panic. "Almost three feet?"

"Yeah. Of course, the drifts are a lot higher. Five or even six feet in some spots."

Feeling unreal, she drifted to the window and rubbed a bit of frost off the glass. Holy cow. The most snow she'd ever seen on the ground before yesterday was a dusting. The aftermath of last night's blizzard was beyond her comprehension. Snow was everywhere, covering the trees, blown up against the back of the barn, piled high like mounds of confectioner's sugar.

"Oh, my God," she breathed. "It's freaking Little House on the Prairie."

"Except without the prairie," Matt said.

"We'll be stuck here eating turnips until spring!"

Chuckling, Matt broke an egg, one handed, into the skillet. "Not quite that long. The county's pretty good with the roads. The plows should make it down here by Sunday at the latest. That's only three days away. Aunt Bea's larder could feed an army until summer. Coffee?"

"Um...sure."

He waved her into a seat and handed her a mug. A few minutes later, two loaded plates landed on the table, bearing fluffy cheese omelets, thick slices of bacon, fried potatoes, and hunks of homemade bread. Casey's mouth started to water.

Matt set an old-fashioned percolator coffee pot on a hot pad in the center of the table and folded his big body into the seat opposite. Casey took a bite of omelet and washed it down with a sip of coffee.

"Delicious," she said.

He looked up. "Thanks."

The aura of morning-after intimacy, even though it

was a morning after nothing, was beyond awkward. Casey cast about for small talk.

"Were you born here in Dutch Gorge?"

"No. Jake and I came to live with Aunt Bea and Uncle Fred when I was four, and he was two. Our sister Mary was a baby. Our parents died in a car crash."

"How sad."

"It was. My father was Uncle Fred's only brother. As for Jake, Mary, and I—we don't remember our parents. Our childhood was here, with Bea and Fred, until we each left for greener pastures."

"Don't you worry about your aunt and uncle now that they're getting older? Living in such an isolated place, I mean."

He put down his fork. "Yes. They refuse to move out. But they're not completely alone—there's a couple who live about a half-mile up the valley who work here during the season. They're spending Christmas with their family in Canada right now. That's why Jake and I are here, to help out with the Romance of Christmas weekend. Aunt Bea won't give it up. She just loves to have the house full for the holiday. But as soon as the guests leave on Sunday, we'll close up the house until April."

"Really? Where will Bea and Fred go?"

"They'll drive with me to Boston, and spend the winter at my sister Mary's place. She's married, with three kids, and has a big house. Good thing, too. Neither Jake or I have the room."

"Bea and Fred are lucky to have you to look after them,"

Casey said around a bite of omelet. "I'd hate to think of something happening to them in the winter, with the road closed and no one able to get to them. Are there a lot of storms like yesterday's?"

"It happens," Matt said. "We get a good bit of snow in the gorge. When I was a kid, it seemed the road was closed more often than it was open." He grinned. "Missed a ton of school."

"What happens if someone gets sick? Or hurt?"

"If it's a real emergency, we radio out and the hospital sends a helicopter." He cupped his mug in his palms. "But believe it or not, that only happened once in all my childhood. Jake ran a sled into a tree and broke his arm."

"Oh, my God! How old was he?"

"Seven."

"Wow. That must have been scary."

"Not for me. It was one of the most exciting days of my life. The only way it could have been better is if I'd been the one with the broken arm getting a ride on a helicopter. For years afterward, every time it snowed I tried to break an arm or leg. But I never quite managed it."

Casey laughed. Amazingly, she was starting to relax. Looking down at her plate, she realized she'd eaten almost everything on it, and her mug was empty, too.

"Your poor aunt," she said, reaching for the coffee pot. "It sounds like you and your brother—oh!"

Her fingers slipped on the handle. The pot tipped with a thud. Casey watched in horror as the battered aluminum top flew off, sending coffee pouring across the table and into Matt's lap.

"Ow!" He leapt to his feet, swatting at his pants with his napkin. "F—" He swallowed. "I mean, *damn*, that's hot."

"Oh, God! I'm so sorry. I'm such a klutz!"

Casey was on her feet too, wishing the floor would open up and swallow her. She came around the table, thrusting her napkin in the general direction of Matt's groin. He grabbed her hand just before it landed on his crotch.

She jerked back, face flooding with heat. "I'm sorry," she repeated weakly.

"Wow," he said, shaking out his wet napkin. The front of his pants were soaked. "Your sister wasn't kidding. You are clumsy." He started to laugh. "You're a walking disaster."

Casey flushed hotter than the coffee. Could she just shrivel up and die now? Please?

"My fingers slipped on the handle when I tried to pick it up," she said lamely.

"That'll be a lesson to me," he said. "Never let your cup go empty."

She covered her face with the napkin. "Oh, God, I—"

"Listen." He tugged the cloth away. His finger brushed her cheek.

Her eyes flew open.

"Don't worry about it," he said. "I'll live. But I've got to change. And then I need to gas up the snow blower and see about clearing a path to the house."

He crossed to the wardrobe and pulled out clean jeans,

shirt and underwear. Tossing the clothes on the bed, he bent to unlace his boots.

Then his hands went to his belt. "You might want to turn your back." He met her startled eyes and grinned. "Or maybe not?"

Casey quickly averted her eyes. "You're going to..." She nearly choked. "...change? Out here?"

"Bathroom's too small. I'm sure you noticed."

"Um...yeah. I guess it is." She spun around, fingers gripping the edge of the table. "Sure. No problem. Go ahead."

"Thanks."

She heard him unbuckle his belt. Listened as he shucked off his jeans. Shrugged out of his shirt. Stepped out of his underwear.

And she saw it all, too. In full frontal glory. Reflected in shiny window glass.

She sucked in a breath as Matt turned to grab his clean clothes off the bed. Damn, but he had an excellent butt. She knew she was acting like some kind of pervert, ogling his reflection. But she couldn't quite bring herself to look away.

Until he looked up, met her gaze in the window, and waved.

***

"So how was your night with Emma?" Matt asked as he and Jake set up the brunch buffet. For the moment, they were alone. Aunt Bea was in the kitchen, mixing up her famous waffle batter. The guests had yet to drift in from the living room.

Jake cut Matt a swift glance. "Fine," he said with uncharacteristic reserve. "How was your night with Klutzy Casey?"

"Don't call her that," Matt said sharply. Then he remembered the way she'd nearly scalded his balls off. "Okay, so she is a bit clumsy. Otherwise, she's not so bad."

Jake positioned the bowls of syrup, nuts, and dried fruits, a smirk on his lips. "But not exactly your usual type."

"Maybe I'm tired of my usual type."

Matt stacked the plates and lit the gas under the trays of eggs and sausage. He could hear the lodge guests, chatting in the living room. Casey wasn't with them, he knew. With all this snow, the only path from the cabin was the one he'd cleared to the kitchen door. He'd have seen her if she'd come in that way.

He wondered if she'd even appear for brunch. She'd already eaten breakfast. But that was hours ago. Was she embarrassed about dousing him with hot coffee? Or irritated that he'd caught her eyeing him in the window reflection? He tried to flirt a little after that, warm her up, but she'd only snorted and given him the cold shoulder.

Maybe she really wasn't interested.

"Seriously," Jake eyed him. "You into Casey? I never would have thought it."

"Just tell me—will Casey be sharing a room with her sister tonight?" He found himself holding his breath, waiting for Jake's answer.

"Not if I can help it. Emma and I had a great time last

night."

Matt's chest eased.

"And you know what else?" Jake continued. "Aunt Bea is right. You should call Emma in for a screen test. She's really something special."

"I told her I would. After the New Year. Get Emma's number for me, okay?"

"Will do."

Aunt Bea came bustling from the kitchen, carrying a large plastic pitcher of waffle batter. She handed it off to Jake. "Ready, boys?"

"You bet," said Jake. But his attention was on Emma, who had just entered the dining room. He thrust the batter at Matt. "Listen, do me a favor."

"Another one?"

"Yeah. Make the waffles."

"Sure thing," Matt said to his brother's back.

Aunt Bea smiled. "Jake is sure taken with that actress."

"I guess so." Matt just hoped his aunt hadn't caught on to the revised sleeping arrangements. She wouldn't be pleased.

But Bea only wiped her hands on her apron and cast a critical eye over the buffet. "Perfect. I'll just tell the guests to come in."

An uncomfortable sensation rose in Matt's chest. As he kept the waffle iron sizzling, his gaze kept returning to Casey's sister. Emma was flirting with Jake, touching his arm and letting him feed her from his plate. Wasn't she thinking about her sister at all?

The meal was almost over by the time Casey finally appeared. Matt tried to catch her attention, but she wouldn't meet his gaze. Her eyes were fixed on her sister, her lips pressed into a straight, angry line.

Matt found himself wondering what Casey looked like with a smile on her face. Oh, not one of those tight little grimaces he'd managed to coax out of her so far. No, he'd really like to see a wide, unrestrained grin. And laughter, the kind she couldn't stop.

And he'd like to be the cause of it.

***

"Emma," Casey hissed the instant Jake left the table to clear the brunch dishes. She slid into the seat he'd reluctantly vacated. "What the hell did you think you were doing last night?"

Emma's gaze lingered on the doorway to the kitchen, through which Jake had just disappeared. She sighed happily. "More than I ever did with Todd, that's for damn sure."

"Emma—"

"The man is a dream, Case. An absolute dream." Emma's smile was brilliant, and her eyes held no hint of their sisterly spats of the day before. Casey only wished she could forgive and forget as easily. But unfortunately, the night hadn't worked out quite so well for her as it had for Emma.

"He's so nice. And funny, too," Emma went on. "He's a musician, a keyboardist, did you know that?"

"Great. Sounds like a real stable job."

Emma ignored the jab. "He lives in Boston, and his band's called "Shake It Up." They play clubs and parties all over New England." Her smiled widened. "And now I feel like I should thank you for being so nasty to me yesterday. I might never have hooked up with Jake otherwise."

"You never should have, anyway," Casey said in a furious whisper. "I still can't believe you locked me out of our room so you could sleep with Jake. For God's sake, Emma, you just met the man yesterday, and you just broke up with Todd two days before that. Would it kill you to take a week off between sex partners once in a while?"

Emma blinked, her smile fading. "Why should I? Just to make up for the years you take off between men? No, I don't think so."

"Now who's being nasty?" Casey said, her voice cracking a little. Her throat had gone suddenly raw. She blinked, hot tears pressing her eyelids.

Emma caught Casey's hand. "Oh, God, Case, I'm sorry. I never should have said that. I love you, you know that. But...you can't deny it's been ages since you've...well, you know."

"The trouble is, Emma, I just don't connect with men as easily as you do. I'm not pretty enough to catch a guy's attention, and I suck at flirting."

"Oh, Casey, that's nonsense. You are pretty, especially when you bother to put on a little make-up. And you have a great personality. You could catch a wonderful guy. What about Matt? He's hot. And Jake said you spent the night with him in some romantic cabin in the woods."

"Only because there was nowhere else he could put a paying guest who was locked out of her room by her own sister. Believe me. It's not like he wanted to spend the night with me."

"But still," Emma persisted, "a cabin in the snowy woods? A man and woman forced to spend the whole long, cold, wintery night together? Major romance potential, no matter how it got started. So tell me, how did it go?"

"How do you think it went? Horrible. My computer and phone both died before midnight, and I spilled hot coffee all over him this morning."

"Oh, Casey," Emma said, laughing. "Leave it to you. You got a hot guy practically held captive, and first you ignore him, then you try to land him in the hospital."

"You don't have to spell it out for me," Casey muttered. "I was there, remember? And I looked a fright. It's a wonder I didn't scare him into the next county."

"From what I can tell, he's still interested, despite the danger. He can hardly take his eyes off you."

"Probably so he can be ready to duck if I get too close. And how do you know, anyway? You weren't looking at Matt. You were too busy with Jake."

"That's how I know. Jake said Matt's really into you."

"Oh, please," Casey said. "Guys who look like Matt Van der Staappen do not get hot for women who look like me."

"That's so not true. I'm telling you, Case, you can hook that man and reel him in. Tonight."

"Emma! He's not a fish."

Emma leaned back in her chair. "Maybe not, but Jake

told me Matt wants another night with you. And I want another night with Jake. So don't bother bringing your duffel back to the room."

Casey gasped. "No way. You are not locking me out again tonight."

Emma smiled. "Just watch me."

Chapter Six

"Snowshoeing? In twenty freaking degrees? I don't think so."

Matt decided to ignore Casey's protest. "You'll need a warmer coat. But I'm sure Aunt Bea has something you can borrow. She keeps a few things on hand for city guests who don't know any better."

Casey settled herself more firmly in the overstuffed armchair, and shook her curls. "No. Forget it. I'm not leaving this room. Or this fire."

"It's a long time until dinner," Matt pointed out. "And everyone else is either ice skating, building snowmen, or making love." He smiled as her color rose. "And I know you're only pretending to read that magazine." Unless she'd recently discovered a passion for fishing. "Come on. Go snowshoeing with me. It'll be fun. I promise."

"I don't see how strapping oversized tennis rackets to your feet and wading through mounds of snow in the freezing cold can be any kind of fun."

"Don't knock it 'till you've tried it."

She glared up at him. "No."

He plucked the magazine from her fingers and tossed it on the floor. Grabbing her wrists, he pulled her bodily from the chair. She stumbled, falling against him, her breasts squashed against his chest. His body tensed as his hands ran up her back.

She found her balance and backed off a few inches. "Please?"

He held out a hand and gave her his most winning smile, despite the voice in his head that urged him to give up. He had never in his life worked this hard for a woman's attention. Maybe that was part of the reason he just couldn't let go. "It's my job to entertain the guests."

"You can't really want to entertain me."

"Why not?"

"Because...because it's not necessary. I'm perfectly happy staying inside."

"You're perfectly bored out of your skull."

She eyed his outstretched hand. Then she sighed. "You're not going to take no for an answer, are you?"

"Nope."

"Oh, all right, then. I'll go. But if I die of hypothermia, it's all on you."

"I'll take my chances," he said.

***

Matt caught Casey's gaze and held it. "Open your legs wider."

He loved that crimson blush creeping up from beneath Casey's borrowed scarf. "Or you'll fall flat on your face," he added.

Ducking her head, Casey looked down and shifted her snowshoes a couple inches farther apart. Her curls peeked from the fur-lined hood of Aunt Bea's old parka. "I don't know about this," she grumbled.

Production Title: Inuit Nights. Florida girl gets lost in the wilds of Alaska. Lonely trapper offers to share his fire...

Jesus. He had to get a grip. Now he was casting himself into imaginary scripts. He'd never done that before.

She eyed the snow drifts on either side of the shoveled path behind the farmhouse. "You're really sure I won't sink if I try to climb that stuff?"

"Absolutely sure," he said.

He snagged her hand and tugged her up the snowy incline. The new snow squeaked under their snowshoes, but, as Matt had predicted, held their weight easily. As they reached the top of the drift, she shook her hand out of his. He glanced over at her. She was looking down at her feet.

"Wow," she said, taking another step forward. "It really does work. Like walking on water."

"Which, I suppose, technically, it is," he said. "Let's go, then. Up the valley." He started walking north. After brief hesitation, she followed.

"I just don't know why you asked me to do this with you," she said after a while.

"I wanted some exercise. And you were bored."

"We won't be out here very long, will we?"

He shot her a glance over his shoulder. "You know, you're always in such a hurry to get rid of me. I'm beginning to think you don't like me."

"Don't like—" She paused, then tucked her chin and resumed her hike. "You can't be serious. I...I like you just fine. It's just that...I'm Klutzy Casey, remember? You'll probably spend half the afternoon pulling me out of snow banks."

"Hey," he said, catching her chin with one gloved finger. "I wouldn't mind."

Her eyes widened, then she ducked her head. "And I'm worried about Emma," she continued. "My sister falls into relationships so quickly. I don't think it's good for her."

Matt wasn't buying it. "Emma strikes me as the kind of woman who has no problem managing her love life."

A touch of defensiveness crept into her voice. "That doesn't mean I don't worry about her."

He forged a trail through the new snow, following the edge of the forest, the mountain rising steeply to his left. In the slice of sky above the gorge, snow clouds were beginning to break up. Blue sky showed through the cracks.

"You're Emma's sister, not her mother," he said. "And she's a grown woman, not a girl."

Casey's next step kicked up some loose powder. "Maybe so, but I've been looking after her for so long. Our mother died when she was five."

"How old were you?"

"Twelve."

"Jesus."

"So after that, it was my job to take care of her. Dad was really no good at it."

"But you were only a kid yourself."

More snow sprayed into the air. "We didn't have any handy relatives to help out. And we couldn't afford a nanny. I didn't mind. In fact, I liked it. It made me feel important, and grown up."

"So you still look after her. You're still the adult, and she's still the kid. You even moved from Florida to New York because you didn't think she could handle life on her own."

"She couldn't have! Not in New York. Her bank account would've been dry in a month. God only knows where she'd be sleeping if not in the apartment I'm paying for."

Matt ducked between two evergreens, releasing a shower of snow. Two displaced chickadees twittered and darted away. He held back a bough while Casey passed through.

"Who looks after you?" he asked.

"I take care of myself."

They hiked on in silence, the trail growing steadily steeper. He inhaled deeply, filling his lungs with air untainted by city smog. He really should find a way to spend more time upstate. His life in the city always seemed more hopeful after a visit home.

He darted a glance at Casey. He was beginning to have hope in that department, too. The hike was a good idea. She was definitely warming to him.

After about a half-hour climb, he reached his destination—a flat ledge where a break in the pines afforded a sweeping view of the valley. Casey halted behind him, pushing her hood back to reveal her wild black curls. Her cheeks were flushed pink with the effort of the climb. She was out of breath, and panting.

Project: Indie Film. Genre: Erotica. Title: Breathless...

He sucked in a breath of his own.

Just then, as if on cue from some unseen director, the sun broke from behind a cloud, flooding the valley with sparkling light.

"Wow." Casey's tone was filled with awe. "What a beautiful view."

"Worth the climb?" Matt asked with feigned casualness.

"Oh, yes. Definitely. Thank you. For insisting I come up here."

She turned and gave him a brilliant smile.

He took it full force in his chest.

Their eyes met and held. After a long moment, the smile wavered, and the light in her eyes dimmed. She gave a self-conscious laugh and turned away.

Not good. In a fit of reflexive desperation, Matt scooped a handful of snow off a nearby bough and tossed it.

It exploded against the back of her head.

"Wha—? Ooh!"

She spun around, shaking her head, curls bouncing, white flakes flinging in every direction. A shudder wracked her body as some of the snow slipped down the back of her neck.

"Oooh! I can't believe you did that!"

Matt was already packing his second handful of snow. He gave her a slow smile as he tossed the snowball from hand to hand.

Her eyes widened. "You wouldn't dare."

"Just watch me." The missile burst against her upper chest, just under her chin.

She sputtered. "Why you—" Dropping into a crouch, she scrabbled to pack her own snowball. But not before he'd tossed a third one.

Her counterassault was two-fisted, and messy. It splattered his stomach and thigh. He retaliated with a quick feint to the left, followed by a well-aimed strike to her chest. She tried to jump backwards, got her snowshoes tangled, and fell on her butt. But she was laughing now, splashing armfuls of snow in his general direction. He bore the brunt of the attack stoically, looming over her as he packed a new ball of snow.

"See this?" he said. "It's going right down your neck."

"No!"

Somehow, despite lying on her back, she'd managed to form a decent snowball. With surprisingly good aim for a southern girl, she flung it directly at his nose.

He tried to dodge, but snowshoes weren't exactly designed for quick movement. It hit him square in the face. With a choked laugh, he lunged for her.

She screamed as he pounced. He tried to take the brunt of his weight on his outstretched arms, but the snow was soft and his hands, poised on either side of her head, sunk through the surface. His body pressed Casey's into the cold, fluffy blanket of white.

He managed enough leverage to roll to one side, taking her with him. He flopped onto his back in the deep depression their bodies had made. Casey sprawled on top of him. Their legs tangled hopelessly, locked tight by their unwieldy snowshoes.

Her head was just below the rim of the snow. His arms were around her waist. She shoved against his chest, trying to lever herself up and off him. She didn't get far. She tried again, her hips shifting and wriggling against his. He felt himself go hard. His hands locked together against her lower back. When she tried a third time to get up, he didn't give her so much as an inch.

He watched her face, and saw the exact moment she realized he was pulling her down rather than helping her up. He waited, his breath barely moving in his lungs, frozen with anticipation. If she really didn't want him, now would be the time to let him know.

She held herself rigid for an instant, her gaze locked with his. He could drown, he thought, in the dark of her eyes. Her eyelashes were thick, and very long. They fluttered downward, and a breath of white-puff air escaped her lips.

She brought her hand up, and tentatively brushed her fingers over the stubble on his chin.

It was all the encouragement he needed.

His hands slid up her back, over her shoulder blades, to settle behind her head. Slowly, he urged her mouth down to his.

***

This is not the sort of thing that happens to me.

This was the kind of thing, Casey thought, that happened to Emma. Emma was the impulsive sister. The beautiful sister. The sister who inspired men to lust on a regular basis.

Casey was the practical one, the smart one, the industrious one. The sister men overlooked.

Matt wasn't overlooking her.

Not by a long shot. His lips were warm, brushed with cool snow. His body was hard and heavy, pressing her down into the snow as his mouth worked magic. She shifted. He froze for a beat, as if he expected her to push him away. Instead she aligned her body more perfectly with his. His arms tightened.

A growl vibrated in his throat. His kiss turned urgent, his lips parting hers, his tongue stroking. And then, somehow, he'd unzipped her coat and was slipping his hands inside. What had happened to his gloves? He palmed her breast, his hand sliding over her sweater, his thumb teasing the peak of her nipple beneath the thin knit fabric. A jolt of electricity zinged through her body.

She felt her insides melting. She'd fallen with her legs on either side of Matt's right thigh; she felt him flex, hard muscle pressing against the sweet spot between her legs. His erection ground against her lower belly, hard and insistent—even through layers of clothing.

"My God, Casey."

His fingers were doing something clever. She arched into the sensation. One of his hands stole around to cup her bottom. He pulled her down, against him, urging, coaxing. God, it felt good.

Too good? There was some reason, she thought, why this wasn't the greatest idea. But Casey's body, in soaking up the sensations flowing through it, had shoved her logical mind into some dark corner of her brain. She couldn't quite work the reason why she should stop.

He tugged up her sweater, insinuating cool fingers against her bare skin. They skated up, taking her sweater with them. Cold air brushed goosebumps across her abdomen. In the next instant, her bra went slack.

His mouth covered her nipple, suckling. Sensation curled, hot and aching, in her chest and belly. She cradled his head against her breast and closed her eyes. He fumbled at the snap on her jeans. His fingers slipped inside, touching her, and she gasped.

This wasn't real. It couldn't be. She felt as if she was outside herself, hovering about ten feet above her body, looking down at a man and woman about to make love in the snow.

How could that woman be her? Had the Casey she'd been all her life vanished that quickly? Or was she so desperate for male attention that she melted for the first hot guy to make a move? Was she so starved for sex she was willing to do it right here in the snow, with a guy she barely knew? A ridiculously hot guy who was hitting on the only unattached female in a snowbound resort?

Her brain and her body abruptly reunited.

She jerked backward, shoving against Matt's chest. She must have caught him off-guard, because she broke his grip easily. Cool air rushed between them. She felt the loss of contact like the twist of a knife in her gut; for an instant, she almost threw herself back on top of him. Their gazes met. His eyes showed his confusion. Hers, she was sure, revealed full-blown panic.

She tried to get off him, but only ended up falling sideways, widening the snow cave they'd created with their bodies. She kicked, trying to untangle their legs.

"Hey." He reached out and grabbed her arm.

"No. Let me go." She flailed at his arm with her fist.

"Whoa. Take it easy." He dropped his arms to his sides. "I'm not trying to do anything you don't want. If you don't want me to touch you, I won't."

She paused, panting. What was she doing? What was she afraid of? She hardly knew.

"I...I'm sorry," she said, finally freeing her legs. She flopped onto her side, panting from the effort. "I...know that. I just started thinking..."

His expression was inscrutable. "Maybe you think too much. Did you ever think of that?"

She was torn between laughter and acute embarrassment. "Or maybe I should have started thinking earlier, before we started this."

She crawled out of the hole and struggled to her feet. He followed her, saying nothing while she hooked her bra and zipped her borrowed coat up to her chin.

"I didn't mean to offend you," he said in a low voice. "I thought..." His color heightened. "I thought maybe you wouldn't mind if I kissed you."

"I didn't mind." Her voice was shaking. He must think she was an idiot. How could she explain? She didn't quite understand herself. "At first. But then, when you... It's just that I'm not..."

"Used to men pawing you in the snow?"

She closed her eyes and sighed. "Used to men pawing me at all. I don't date much."

"Then the men you know must be idiots."

She opened her eyes and managed a half-laugh. "Just the opposite, actually. The guys I know are brilliant computer geeks."

"Smart guys can be idiots, too."

"And they can be married. Which is what most of the men I work with are."

"You must know some single guys. Through Emma?"

"The actors, you mean? And even worse, the agents? Please. Not my type."

His jaw tightened. "Not smart enough for you? Or is it just all the shallowness you object to?"

Her legs were cold. She busied herself with swatting the snow off her jeans.

"I know you heard me badmouthing Emma's friends before. But the truth is, I just don't click with the men she knows. They're all too good-looking, too confident, too extroverted. A guy like that wouldn't give me a second look."

"That's his loss, then. I'm way past giving you a second look. In fact, I think I've lost count."

"Yes, but that's only because of this place."

"What do you mean, this place?"

"This situation," she explained. "I'm the only available woman in the lodge, and you were all but forced to offer me the couch in your cabin."

"You can't possibly believe that. Did you see anyone holding a gun to my back when I asked you to go snowshoeing?"

"No," she conceded. "But be honest. If you passed me on the street, or met me at a party surrounded by twenty or so women as beautiful as Emma, would you even notice me?"

"Of course," he said. But not before he'd hesitated just a split second.

"No," Casey said. "You wouldn't."

He frowned down at her. "Then I'd be the idiot. Because you're a very attractive woman."

"No. Emma's the attractive one. She causes whiplash every time she walks down the street."

He studied her, his expression intent. It felt as if he were looking under her skin. She wondered what he saw.

"Your sister is stunning, Casey. And yes, I won't lie to you, I noticed her first."

Why did his words hurt? They were only the truth.

"But that doesn't mean you're not pretty. But it feels that way to you, doesn't it? It must be hard, living in her shadow."

She rubbed her arms. The chill was seeping into her bones. She wanted to be back in the lodge, in her chair in front of the fire, with the fishing magazine she didn't want to read. She wished she had never left.

"Emma's my sister. I love her."

"But you can't help but be jealous."

"No. I'm not. I'm—"

"Of course you are. Sometimes. It's nothing to be ashamed of. I love Jake, but that doesn't stop me from envying him."

She blinked. "You're envious of Jake? But why?"

Now he was the one who seemed embarrassed. He rubbed the back of his neck. "It's hard to explain. Jake's always been...I don't know...more real than I am."

"That makes no sense."

"It does to me. With Jake, what you see is what you get. He doesn't have a self-conscious bone in his body. Me...I find it hard to show myself to the world. I always want a buffer. A mask." He exhaled. "Do you have any idea what I mean?"

"I...yes. Yes, I do."

An understatement. She knew exactly what he meant. She'd been hiding herself all her life.

"Tell me something, Casey. If you met me at a party, and found out that I barely finished high school, would you give me a second glance? Or would you figure I was someone you didn't want to know?"

She didn't answer. After a moment, he cleared his throat. "I thought so." He paused. "Ready to head back?"

She touched his arm. "You're right. If I'd met you in New York, at one of Emma's parties, I wouldn't have talked to you. But not because you didn't go to college. Because you're just too damn good-looking."

He shot her a look. "Usually, women like that."

She just shrugged and started walking.

Single file, they retraced their trail back to the valley floor. Matt didn't speak until they turned to follow the wider trail along the tree line.

"You know, when I left Dutch Gorge, I went straight to New York City. Just like Emma. I had this idea I was going to be an actor."

"No. You're kidding me."

"I'm not. And I did score some jobs. Modeling, at first. Magazine ads, and then some television. I even managed to land a few off-Broadway roles before I quit. So I really would fit in quite well with your sister's friends." He paused. "The ones you don't like."

Her stomach gave a lurch. "Why did you give it up? The acting, I mean. It sounds like you were a lot more successful than Emma's been."

He shrugged. "Maybe. But acting's an insane way to make a living. I'm a perfectionist, and I just wasn't as good at it as I thought I should be. So after a few years, I gave up and...and moved on. But I've found that in a way, acting never gave me up. It's so much easier for me to see life...like a theater production, I suppose. It feels that way much of the time, anyway."

They'd reached the clearing in back of the barn. Matt

stopped, and caught Casey's gloved hand. "But last night, and today...I find I don't want to play a part. I know this is quick, Casey, and it doesn't seem like we're two people who would normally get together, but...it feels right, being with you. It feels real. And I have to tell you, I'm very, very glad your sister is going to lock you out of your room again tonight."

She looked up at him, her heart tripping, the bottom of her stomach falling, falling, falling.

"What about you?"

Her eyes had gone wide. "Me? I...I don't know." She swallowed. "Just what is it that you're asking me, Matt?"

He dragged a hand through his hair. "I guess...whatever you want me to ask. Nothing more than that."

A breeze caught a curl and flung it into her eyes. He smiled, and tucked it behind her ear.

Leaning forward, he brushed a soft kiss on her lips.

"You can give me your answer tonight."

Chapter Seven

They returned to the lodge to find the rest of the guests relaxing with hot chocolate and spiked eggnog. Casey spotted Jake and Emma entwined under a ball of mistletoe.

Matt cleared his throat, prompting them to come up for air, to the general amusement of the other guests. Emma, eyes dancing, flashed Casey an unrepentant grin. Jake reached up and snapped a twig from the mistletoe ball. He dangled it over Casey's head.

"Your turn," he said. "Come on, Matt. Let's see what you've got. Or should I do the honors myself?"

"Don't you dare."

Before Casey quite knew what had happened, Matt had spun her around and dragged her against the hard wall of his chest. His lips covered hers, sending a sweet twist of desire down her body. For a moment, she clung to him, almost forgetting where she was, until a round of laughter and applause snapped her back to her senses.

She tore her lips away. Matt leaned in and whispered against her ear. "Lots more where that came from."

He straightened as Jake clapped him on the back and

gave him some good-natured ribbing. Matt grinned and offered an insult in return. Soon after, when the brothers headed to the kitchen to prep for dinner, Emma wasted no time in hauling Casey to a quiet spot near the Christmas tree.

"Soooo." Her eyes danced. "Things are happening for you, too! Way to go, Case. I'm so glad. You'll be putting that romantic little cabin to good use tonight, I bet."

Casey touched a spun glass snowman ornament. "No, Emma, I won't be. It's way too soon."

"I think not. Did you catch that look Matt gave you on his way out? I seriously expected this tree to go up in flames. That man is deeply in lust. And if he's even half as good as his brother…" Emma rolled her eyes and exhaled a long, satisfied sigh. "You are in for one fantastic night."

"Emma, for God's sake, be quiet! Or at least, keep your voice down."

Casey's sister flicked a hand. "Oh relax. No one's listening."

"They will be if you insist on broadcasting rave reviews of Jake's talents."

"Okay, then. Forget Jake's talents, many though they are. Let's hear about Matt. What's going on between you two?"

"Nothing."

Emma eyed her. "You're lying. I can always tell. Something happened on that little hike you took this afternoon, didn't it?"

"Oh, all right. Something did happen. But it was no big

deal. He kissed me." *And then we did a bit more than kiss.* Heat crept up her neck and into her cheeks.

And damn it, Emma noticed. "You're blushing, Casey!" A smile tugged at her lips. "Just for a kiss? Must have been a good one."

"Em. It's none of your business."

"You know, I don't agree. You're my sister. Your business is my business."

"Forget it," Casey said flatly.

"Not likely! You're always so full of advice. Why shouldn't I be the one to give out a tip or two once in a while? And you have to admit, this is my area of expertise. So tell me, Case. Just how long has it been since you've had sex? Ages, right?"

"Emma! I don't ask details about your sex life."

"Just answer the question."

Casey sighed. "Okay. Three years, all right? With Doug. You remember him, right?"

"That long?" The horror in Emma's eyes was unfeigned. "And with that loser? Holy crap, Casey. No wonder you're so uptight. That settles it. You have to sleep with Matt. Tonight. Your mental health depends on it."

"If there's anything affecting my mental health," Casey retorted, "it's my sister. Not the fact that I don't want to jump into bed with a guy I barely know."

Liar, a little voice inside her skull taunted.

"But you like the guy," Emma persisted. "A lot. Admit it."

"So what if I do? That doesn't change the fact that I

just met him yesterday."

"Who cares when you met him? Does he make your insides melt?"

Casey's shoulders slumped. "Yes."

"And are you an independent, adult woman?"

"That's neither here nor there. It would never work. Matt is just too...too hot."

Emma rolled her eyes. "Girl, there is no such thing."

"Honestly, Emma, look at him. Then look at me."

"You look fine," Emma said. "Or at least, you would if you believed in yourself. Attitude counts more than anything."

"That's easy for you to say," Casey muttered.

Emma huffed out a breath. "It's easy to say because it's true! Geez, Case, the guy already wants you. All you have to do is loosen up and give him a little encouragement." She nudged Casey in the ribs. "I know you want to. I can see it in your eyes."

A little shiver ran up Casey's spine. Emma was right. She did want to.

There. She'd admitted it. At least to herself.

She cleared her throat. "I'll think about it, okay?"

"Oh, Casey," Emma said, shaking her head. "For someone who's so smart, you really are dumb sometimes. Thinking is exactly what you shouldn't do. Promise me. When Matt asks, don't think. Go with your heart."

***

Matt, wearing a white chef's apron, carved a haunch of roast venison for Christmas Eve dinner. Jake emerged from the kitchen, a half-dozen platters of potatoes and vegetables balanced on his arms.

"Oh!" Emma jumped up. "Let me help, before it all ends on the floor."

The platters were soon relayed down the table and the guests all seated. Aunt Bea carried in a tray of pastries while Uncle Fred lit a row of candles down the center of the table. Casey was all too aware of Matt sliding into his usual seat beside her.

Uncle Fred bowed his head and said the blessing.

"A fine Christmas Eve, with family and new friends." Aunt Bea beamed down the table after her husband's hearty "Amen." "

Dinner and conversation began in earnest. Casey eyed the slice of venison on her plate.

"Never had it?" Matt guessed.

"No," Casey admitted. She tasted a tiny piece. "Why, it's not so bad."

Matt laughed. "Aunt Bea will be pleased to hear it. You know, Jake and I ate venison all the time when we were kids. Uncle Fred's a good shot, and Aunt Bea refused to let any meat he brought home go to waste. Broiled, stewed, dried...you name it, she's got a recipe."

After the dinner dishes were cleared, pots of tea were poured, and the tray of Dutch pastries was moved from the sideboard to the middle of the table.

"*Letterbanket*," Matt explained, placing a tube-shaped pastry on Casey's plate. "Shaped like the letters of the alphabet. Here's a 'C' for you." He took an 'M' for himself.

Casey bit into hers. It was filled with almond paste. "Delicious."

After dessert, Matt and Jake swiftly cleared the table. As the guests finished their coffee and wandered back into the living room, Jake appeared at Emma's side.

"I need you," he declared.

She batted her eyelashes. "Oh, really?"

He grinned. "Not for that. At least, not yet."

He grabbed her hand and tugged her to the piano. Casey, left alone, watched her sister and her new lover bend their heads over a stack of sheet music. They made a handsome couple, Jake's brown hair brushing Emma's blonde head. Their body language was so in tune, and their laughter was genuine. It was as if they'd known each other for years, rather than just a day.

Aunt Bea and Uncle Fred began herding the guests toward the piano. "Time for carols," Aunt Bea explained. "You too, dear," she said when Casey hung back from the rest.

Reluctantly, Casey joined the outer fringe of the group. Everyone in the lodge was present, except Matt. Was he still in the kitchen, tackling the clean-up on his own?

Jake settled on the piano bench. Emma stood at his side, poised to turn pages.

"Sing loud," he told her with a wink.

He struck the opening chord to *Deck the Halls*. Emma added her beautiful voice, and the other guests soon joined in. The farmhouse reverberated with song.

Jake's fingers flew over the keys. He really was a

talented pianist, Casey mused. Maybe his musical career wasn't as frivolous a pursuit as she'd assumed. He kept song after song coming, with hardly a pause in between. But Casey found her attention straying. She couldn't get Matt—and the long night ahead—out of her mind. He'd put the ball firmly in her court. *I'll ask whatever you want me to ask*, he'd said.

The problem was, what was that?

Emma's advice spun circles in her head. Should she really throw caution to the wind? Listen to her heart? Even if Casey wanted to, she was hardly sure what her heart was saying. The flapping butterfly wings in her stomach were drowning it out.

Jake struck the last plaintive chord to *God Rest Ye Merry Gentlemen*. Then his touch softened on the opening bars of *What Child is This?* All other voices fell away as Emma's sweet soprano filled the air.

A rush of pride filled Casey's chest. Her sister was as talented as she was beautiful, and, despite her tendency to act first and think later, she had a good heart. And maybe, on occasion, she was wise, too. Emma had only met Jake yesterday, but he was already enthralled. Could Casey dare hope Matt felt the same way?

Emma held the final, lingering note until it evaporated into the air. A heartbeat of silence ensued, followed by hearty applause and enthusiastic praise.

"Beautiful," Uncle Fred declared. "Truly beautiful."

Aunt Bea smiled. "With talent like that, dear, I'm sure you'll find yourself on Broadway someday."

"I can only hope," Emma sighed.

Jake and Aunt Bea exchanged a glance. "Oh, I think you can do more than that," he said, shuffling the sheet music. "One last song." He sent Casey a pointed look. "And I want to hear everybody this time. That means you, Casey."

Casey laughed and dutifully joined her voice to a lively arrangement of *Santa Claus is Coming To Town*. As the song drew to a close, a voice boomed from the foyer.

"*Vrolijk Kerstfeest!* Merry Christmas!"

The singing abruptly transformed into a chorus of laughter. "Sinterklaas!" Uncle Fred called. "Welcome!"

A tall old-world Santa Claus, complete with long, curly beard, gold-trimmed red cape, and tall bishop's hat, appeared in the archway under the mistletoe, a sack slung over his shoulder. Aunt Bea went up on her toes to buss his cheek. Santa's blue eyes caught Casey's gaze over the top of Bea's head.

Matt's lips curved into a rueful smile behind his fake beard.

Casey started to laugh.

"Oh, my God," said Emma, elbowing Casey in the ribs. "Matt is one sexy Santa."

He was, Casey had to admit.

"*Vrolijk Kerstfeest!*" Matt slung the pack from his shoulder. "Gather round, ladies. Sinterklaas has something for each one of you."

He presented Aunt Bea with her gift first—a beautiful embroidered shawl. "From your nephews," Sinterklaas told her.

"And now, from the Van der Staappens to their Christmas guests." Matt made a show of rummaging about in his sack, handing out gaily wrapped boxes to the female guests. When he came to Emma and Casey, he looked from one to the other and hesitated. "There's only one left."

"Because I wasn't supposed to be here," Casey said, hiding a twinge of disappointment. "You take it, Emma. It's your vacation."

"Are you sure?"

"Very."

Emma accepted the gift. The paper was gold, with silver stars. "It's heavy," she said, weighing it in her hands.

"Open it," Casey urged.

Emma set the box on the piano, tore open the wrapping, and lifted the lid. "Oh! How beautiful!"

The old-fashioned snow globe was real glass. Inside, flakes of white surrounded a tiny replica of Dutch Lodge. The words "Romance of Christmas 2013" were inscribed on its polished wood base.

Emma inverted the globe and turned it upright again. Snow swirled all around the miniature farmhouse. A glance around the room told Casey the other women had received identical gifts. Everyone were as charmed as she and Emma were.

"Pretty, huh?" Jake said. "Uncle Fred found a local artisan who makes them by hand."

"It's lovely. I think I'll go thank Fred and Bea right now."

"Sure thing," Jake said. They stepped away, leaving Casey alone with Matt.

She smiled. "You know, you make a very nice Santa."

He tugged off his beard and placed it on a nearby table. His bishop's hat joined it. "Sinterklaas," he corrected. "The Dutch version of Santa Claus. Not as fat as the American one. And much more dignified. Normally Uncle Fred does the honors, but this year, I asked him to let me do it."

"Why?"

"Because I wanted Sinterklaas to give you this."

His hand disappeared into the folds of his cape. "It's not wrapped, though, so close your eyes."

A thrill of anticipation ran through Casey. Her lashes swept down. Matt caught her hand and pressed something smooth and cool into her palm.

Her eyes flew open. "Your mystery box! But...I couldn't possibly accept this. It's part of your childhood."

"I haven't opened it in ages, and it really seemed to intrigue you. I'd like you to have it."

She turned the box over, marveling again at the workmanship. "Well...if you're sure?"

"I am."

"Then thank you."

"You're welcome." He seemed uncertain for a moment, as if waiting for her to say or do something else. Finally, he drew a breath. "Do you remember how to open it?"

His voice had dropped to a near whisper. The intimacy sent a jolt of awareness through Casey's senses. "I...I think so." Her fingers searched for the hidden catch. "Let me see..."

She found a small, folded sheet of paper nestled inside.

"Open it," Matt said.

She extracted the paper, her fingers trembling slightly as she unfolded it. There was a single symbol on it. A question mark.

"What's this?"

"A question."

Her eyes collided with his. "What kind of question?"

"Your question. The one you want me to ask." He lifted his hand and cupped the side of her face, tracing the arch of her cheekbone with his thumb. "Do you know what it is yet?"

She closed her eyes and turned her head into his hand, brushing his palm with her lips. Heat gathered low in her belly. She couldn't capture a clear thought in her head—her emotions were too tangled. Desire, fear, anticipation, uncertainty, foreboding, excitement... She was so mixed up over this man she'd just met. And yet, in some strange, primal way, she was drawn to him. Could someone really fall in love that quickly? She didn't know.

His hand slid around to the back of her neck, urging her closer. She went, her eyes still closed. His heavy cape enfolded both of them, shutting the rest of the room out.

Emma had told her to go with her heart. That organ was pounding loudly now, and she knew exactly what it was saying.

She opened her eyes. And was immediately seared by the heat of his gaze. An answering fire flashed through her.

Her knees went weak. She grasped the embroidered edge of his cape as his arm came around her, holding her steady.

"Yes." Her throat was dry. "I know the question I want you to ask."

"Consider it asked," he said. His lips touched hers. "And your answer?"

She felt her heart take a flying leap of faith.

"Yes," she said. "My answer is yes."

Chapter Eight

The walk from the kitchen door to the cabin in the woods passed in a blur. Casey was aware, on an intellectual level, at least, that it was very cold outside. But the hunger in Matt's eyes left room for nothing but slow, dark heat.

His arm around her waist was solid and sure, and it seemed her boots barely skimmed the snow as he hustled her down the path to his cabin. The door swung closed behind them.

He toed off his boots, and left her briefly to light the lamp. Casey removed her own boots, then shrugged out of her coat and hung it on the hook by the door. She rubbed her arms at the sudden loss of warmth as Matt crossed the room to build up the fire, his red velvet cape swirling behind him. He tossed on two logs, then stood against a background shower of sparks.

Casey hadn't moved from her position by the door.

He approached her slowly. "Second thoughts?"

"No." She swallowed hard. "Should there be?"

"I hope not." He caught her hand. "I'm praying there's not."

"I—" She cut off as a low, mournful wail, like a deep, rich foghorn, sounded in the darkness outside the cabin. "What's that?"

Matt smiled. "A Dutch *midwinterhoorn*. It's an ancient custom. Uncle Fred always blows it on Christmas Eve, over the old well in the front yard. It's supposed to chase away evil spirits."

The horn sounded again. "That's lovely." Casey toyed with one of the hand-tooled gold clasps on the front of his cape. "And what about this costume? Is it from Holland? It looks old."

"It's a family heirloom. And yes, it's from The Netherlands. My grandfather brought it with him when he came to America."

"When was that?"

"During the Great Depression. The Netherlands was hit hard. No work to be found and the family was all but starving. Granda had a cousin in New York who helped him emigrate. He brought his wife and two young sons."

"That was your father and Uncle Fred? How old were they?"

"My father was about six, I think. Uncle Fred was an infant."

He unclasped the cape and swung it off his shoulders, draping it over the back of a chair with reverence. "I remember my father wearing this. Not on Christmas, though. On Saint Nicholas Day, the year before he died. It's one of my few memories of him."

He turned back to her, just Matt now, dressed in his

usual jeans and sweater. The fire in the hearth leapt, throwing dancing shadows across his face. Out of the corner of her eye, his double bed loomed large. Casey tried to picture herself in it. With him. The image didn't quite appear.

Despite Emma's pep talk, it was still so hard to believe such a beautiful man really wanted her.

His warm palms descended on her shoulders. "Hey. Stop thinking. Relax."

"I'm not sure I can."

"Casey." His voice was sober as he guided her toward the fire. "I hope you know I'm not going to do anything you don't want me to. In fact, if you want to stop right now... If all you want to do is talk, or play cards, or...whatever, that's all right with me."

She inhaled, for courage. "No. It's not that. It's just that it's been kind of a long time since I..."

God. She could hardly say it. How was she going to *do* it?

A little smile played on his lips. His thumbs played on the bare skin at the neckline of her sweater. "How long?"

She gave a shaky laugh. "You would ask." She tried to look away, but he caught her chin and brought her gaze back to his.

"Three years," she admitted.

"Wow." His lips quirked. "Jesus. I never did it with a virgin before."

She laughed. "Hardly."

His eyes turned serious. "Ever been in love?"

Yes. Since just this afternoon. "No. Not really." She paused. "What about you?"

He gave a half-laugh, and looked away. "Me? Not even close."

The silence that ensued threatened to stretch into awkwardness. With a slight frown, Matt tugged her a few steps backward to the couch. He shoved the blankets she'd used the night before to one side and sat, drawing her down beside him.

He didn't speak. That was good, because as far as Casey was concerned, talking led to thinking, and thinking led to second guessing. Go with your heart, Emma had told her. Was that good advice? Casey's heart was reaching toward Matt, and telling her to let him in.

He exhaled a slow breath and leaned toward her, one arm stretched along the back of the sofa. With his free hand, he fluffed her curls around her face.

"Oh, stop," she laughed, catching his fingers. "I must look like a witch."

"A very sexy witch." His eyes were intent.

Desire unfurled in Casey's chest. The musk of his cologne teased her senses. In a sudden burst of boldness, she slipped her hands under his sweater and shirt and splayed her fingers on his bare skin. His heart thumped against her palms, beating almost as quickly as hers.

He grasped the hem of his sweater and, with one smooth motion, pulled both sweater and shirt over his head. God, but he was solid, his muscles taut under her fingers. His skin was hot, almost burning. Her hands skated up to tangle in the dusting of hair on his chest.

His lips came down on hers, hungry and demanding. She responded with a surging hunger of her own. Her hands slid up and around his neck, and he deepened the kiss, urging her lips apart. He rose over her, pressing her down into the cushions, his erection brushing her thigh. Instinctively, she shifted, opening her legs, cradling him. He froze for a split instant, then his lips slid from her mouth and pressed in an open-mouth kiss against her shoulder.

"God, Casey. I want to see all of you."

He lifted the hem of her sweater and eased it over her head, then went to work on the buttons of the blouse beneath. The shirt was soon gone, along with her bra, almost before she realized what had happened.

He drew back a fraction, his eyes sweeping down her body. She shivered, and fought an urge to cover herself. She was small up top, at least compared to Emma. But if Matt minded, he was hiding it admirably. Only the best actor could have feigned the hot burn of lust in his eyes.

He slid his hands up under her breasts, capturing her gaze and holding it as he brushed his thumbs over her nipples. The exquisite burst of pleasure dragged a moan from her throat.

"No. Don't close your eyes. Let me see you."

She obeyed, feeling even more vulnerable than before.

"You're beautiful," he whispered.

A protest leapt to the tip of her tongue. At the last moment, she swallowed it unsaid. *Attitude,* Emma had said. *Believe in yourself.* Maybe, for once, she should be the sister taking advice, rather than the one dishing it out.

He bent his head to her breast. Her hips came off the couch when his teeth captured one peaked tip on a gentle nibble. His hands went to the waist of her pants, sliding the button from its hole and tugging down the zipper. They slid over her bottom, taking her panties with them. And all the while his mouth was worshipping one breast, then the other.

And then she was completely bare, his mouth trailing kisses between her breasts and down her belly. She gasped when he shifted his weight over the edge of the couch, dropping onto his knees before her. He hooked his arms under her thighs and pulled her to the edge of the couch, parting her legs wide at the same time. His chin brushed her mound. She felt his breath on her most tender skin.

Panic struck. "Oh God. No." She felt unbearably exposed. She'd never— "Matt. Wait. Don't—aaah!"

Her protests dissolved under the hot lash of Matt's tongue. She fisted her hands in his hair, intending to push him away. Then he licked a sweet, perfect stroke and she found herself clutching him closer. She heard a low chuckle, but by that time he'd added his fingers to his sweet torture and she was beyond caring.

She was so close to the edge. So close...

She gasped when he suddenly drew back. "What—?"

His answer was a tight smile. He half-rose, hooking one arm under her knees and the other beneath her shoulder blades. He straightened, lifting her. Trembling, wanting, she wrapped her arms around his neck and pressed her cheek against his chest. His skin was damp. He smelled like sweat, lust, and wood smoke. She inhaled deeply as he covered the distance to his bed in three strides.

He tumbled her down on the rumpled sheets. His heat withdrew as he rummaged in the nightstand drawer. She drank in his profile, anticipation coiling in her belly. The mattress dipped. Matt tossed a wrapped condom down beside her.

Casey's breath left in a whoosh. She hadn't even thought of birth control. God, but her brain was completely scrambled. It was a good thing Matt's was still functioning.

He crawled over her on all fours, and the fire blazed anew between them. She arched toward him, sliding her hands over his chest and stomach, and lower. Taking him in her hands, she stroked hot, velvety skin over hard muscle. Once, twice, three times...

He grabbed her hand, air sawing in and out of his lungs. "Watch it. Not yet."

His thigh sunk between her legs. His eyes were closed, his expression almost one of pain. She could hardly believe she was lying in bed, naked, with a man like him. He was far more than she'd ever dreamed of—when she'd allowed herself to dream at all.

The thought made her resolve fade fast. Was she anything like the woman of Matt's dreams? Impossible. She was the woman who happened to be on hand.

Doubts started crowding in.

"Damn." Matt swore softly. Eyes open now, he dipped his head to nip at her jaw. "Don't leave me, Casey. Please. Whatever you're thinking—stop it."

His teeth snagged her neck and gently bit. Her misgivings wavered. His hands swept down her body. The doubts scattered further. His thigh rode up firmly between her legs, and her brain blanked completely.

And in that oblivion, a spark of confidence rekindled. Without stopping to think, Casey moved against Matt, matching his urgency. She groped for the condom. He supported himself on rigid arms as she covered him.

Both his legs were between hers now, holding her apart as his fingers played wickedly. She scraped her palms on either side of his jaw and drew him down for a kiss. He took her lips with a growl, the tip of his erection sliding into place and pulsing against her wet heat.

"Look at me, Casey."

She did. The expression in his eyes made her breath catch. Her need ratcheted. Her hips tilted upward, inviting, pleading. He held her gaze as he entered her. Slowly. Her hands found the curve of his buttocks; she urged him closer. He flexed his hips and slid deeper. And deeper still.

She bit her lip as he started rocking inside her. Stunning waves of sensation rippled through her body. He was watching her face, his eyes too knowing. Her eyelids fluttered closed.

"No—don't," he whispered. He surged forward, then retreated. On the next stroke, he changed his angle subtly, and hit a spot that made her gasp. "I want to see it in your eyes when you come."

She wanted that, too.

She opened her eyes. Their gazes caught, and their souls seemed to link. Her inner muscles contracted; she felt Matt pulse, deep inside.

He groaned, and moved faster. "God, Casey. You feel...so good. So damn right."

"So do you." A slow smile curved her lips. "Sinterklaas."

His half-laugh dissolved into a groan as his cadence quickened even more. *Good* dissolved into something much, much, better as his strokes came harder, and faster, and harder still. Casey clutched Matt's shoulders as the peak rushed her.

Then she was over the edge, gasping his name, flying free. Matt's arms wrapped firmly around her torso, drawing her flat against his damp skin. His lips pressed to the crook of her neck. His pleasure-roughened growl vibrated against her skin as his own orgasm hit.

Afterwards, Casey floated down to earth without a single doubt.

At least for now.

Chapter Nine

Dawn came and went. It was the best damn Christmas morning Matt had had in years. He didn't even bother getting out of bed, except once, to build up the fire.

He slid back under the quilt as quickly as he could. Casey was curled up on her side, hugging an extra pillow. There were about a thousand snarls in her hair. He smiled. He'd put just about every one of them there.

He slid under the quilt and propped himself up on his elbow, facing her. She had a hickey on her neck. Looking at it got him hot all over again. The sex last night had been incredible. Casey had been incredible.

If he'd met her in the city, he wouldn't have given her a second look. Now he was wondering what she saw in him. And all because he was a different man here in the gorge than he was in the city.

He'd always known there was a part of himself he'd abandoned when he left his childhood home to find his way in the world. What he hadn't known was that it had been here all that time, waiting for him to find his way back.

But he wasn't staying in this perfect world, was he? In

a few days, he'd return to his life in the city, where he worked long hours, made heartless decisions, played complicated networking games. Where he wasn't a laid back, simple-pleasures kind of guy. And the truth was, he liked his career and city life. His New York self was part of him, too. The bigger part now. He wasn't about to leave it all to return to his roots permanently.

His peaceful mood dimmed. He'd avoided telling Casey about his life outside Dutch Gorge. She'd made it clear what she thought about his world. Would she reconsider now that they'd slept together? Would she even like the man he was in the city?

Damn. His morning-after glow was shot to hell. And Aunt Bea would be needing him soon in the kitchen. Sliding carefully out of bed, he showered and dressed. He was lacing up his boots when Casey stirred and sat up, blinking sleep from her eyes.

"Matt?"

"Over here," he said. "Merry Christmas."

"Oh! It is Christmas, isn't it?" Her shy smile squeezed his insides. "Merry Christmas." Her gaze went to the window. "It's getting light out. Kinda. What time is it?"

"Daylight comes late in the gorge this time of year. It's almost eight."

"And you're going out?"

"Yeah. Aunt Bea'll be expecting me in the kitchen." He hesitated. "I'll be busy today. You won't be seeing much of me before dinner. That's at three, by the way. But there'll be a cold breakfast spread in the dining room at ten. You can sleep in until then."

"Or I could help you and Aunt Bea," She started to get out of the bed, then stopped abruptly, jerking the covers back over her nude body. "Um…"

Oh, man. Just one glimpse and he wanted to dive back into bed, and to hell with the city and the future. They were both here in the gorge now, weren't they? For a couple more days, anyway.

Unfortunately, he had work to do. He pulled on his coat. "Don't even bother offering to help in the kitchen. You're a lodge guest. Aunt Bea wouldn't let you lift a finger."

"But—"

He leaned over the bed and gave her a quick kiss. "Do me a favor. Get a couple extra hours of sleep. Believe me, you're going to need it tonight."

"Why? What's tonight?"

He gave her a slow smile. "Tonight's when I get you back into that bed."

***

Casey passed the next two days in a happy haze. More than once, she wondered when she was going to wake up and find out it was all a dream.

Not that she wanted to wake up. No way. She was beginning to believe that Dutch Lodge was a little bit magical, like a wintery Shangri-La or something. She even found herself wishing for another blizzard. One that would keep the roads closed and her computer unplugged indefinitely.

Matt's Uncle Fred led a short prayer service before Christmas brunch, since the roads to the local churches were still impassable. Christmas afternoon, while Matt and Jake were occupied in the kitchen, Casey helped Emma and the rest of the lodge guests build a giant snowman in the front yard. Afterwards, the whole group stomped back into the house, laughing and chatting, to roast chestnuts and drink hot cider.

Christmas dinner was an elaborate affair, featuring roast goose and *boterkoek*, or almond butter cake. After dinner Uncle Fred told traditional Dutch stories by the hearth.

After Bea and Fred had said their goodnights, and the fire had burned low, Jake tugged Emma up the stairs. Casey and Matt, arms entwined, made their way through the snow to the cabin. They made love half the night, and woke to sun streaming through their windows.

The day after Christmas brought sled races, snow angels, and hot chocolate. Casey even let Matt talk her into a pair of ice skates. She clung to him, laughing, as he hauled her around the frozen lake. And she wished the weekend would never end.

But early Sunday morning, the outside world intruded, in the form of a pair of snowplows grinding down the road leading out of the gorge. The harsh reverberation of their engines shattered Casey's fairy-tale reverie.

Today was the day she and Emma returned to the city.

Breakfast came early; immediately after, Matt and Jake attacked the lodge parking lot with snow blower and shovels. Casey returned to the cabin alone, to gather her things and shove them into her duffle.

She packed the mystery box last. Zipping the bag, she sat on the rumpled bed and hugged Matt's pillow. His scent lingered; she inhaled deeply. Then, with one last look around, she hefted her duffel and laptop and headed to the lodge.

Emma was sitting alone at the dining room table, sipping coffee. Casey poured a cup and joined her.

"Jake asked me to come up to Boston for New Year's," Casey's sister informed her. "What about you and Matt? Did you make plans?"

"No." Casey took more care than necessary spooning sugar into her cup. Somehow, as if by silent agreement, she and Matt hadn't talked about what would happen between them after today. And what did that mean? She didn't want to face it. "Matt didn't say anything about New Year's Eve. It doesn't matter. I'll be working anyway."

If she still had a job after dropping off the face of the planet for four days.

Emma made a face. "Working on New Year's Eve is downright inhuman. I hope they're paying you triple time. I guess you can see Matt afterwards."

"I don't know," Casey said, trying to ignore an uneasy feeling in her gut. "Maybe, but then again...well, the thing is, Matt and I might not keep seeing each other. I mean, I'm not really into long distance relationships."

"What long distance? From the Village to the Upper West Side?"

Casey went still. "What are you talking about? Matt lives in Boston."

Emma looked at her oddly. "No, he doesn't. Jake and his sister live in Boston. Matt lives in Manhattan. He has a business there or something."

"No. That can't be. He said he lived—" She hesitated, considering. "No. Actually, he never said anything about where he lived. I just assumed he lived in Boston, because he talked about driving there today with his aunt and uncle. But he was talking about driving to his sister's house, wasn't he?"

Emma laughed. "I guess you two were so busy with other things you forgot about exchanging addresses."

Casey frowned into her coffee. "I guess."

"Oh, don't worry. He'll call. I'd put money on it. Give him our number before we leave."

"Yeah," Casey said. "I will." But she wasn't at all sure Emma would win her bet.

Chapter Ten

The Diva Diamonds New Year's Eve deadline was breathing down Casey's neck like a rabid tiger. Her team had under twenty-four hours to get everything in place. The past few days, she'd worked like a maniac. After her latest thirty-hour stint, she'd dragged her sorry carcass home to catch a few hours of sleep. She took a fortifying swig of coffee. Time to head back into the pit. It was going to be one hell of a night.

She was lucky she still had her job. Her panicked colleagues had covered for her during her days offline, wondering where the hell she'd gone. They'd been immensely relieved when she'd resurfaced. With a little added push, the project would come together tomorrow night at nine, right on schedule. And everything would be fine.

But everything didn't feel fine. It just felt...wrong. Her coffee...her apartment...her job...

Her life.

But that was ridiculous. Her life wasn't wrong. It was fine. At least, it had been fine two weeks ago. And nothing was really different now. Therefore, logically, her life was still fine.

Except that it wasn't.

Her life might be the same, but she wasn't. She was the one who had changed. Into an idiot. And all because of a man.

Pathetic.

She didn't want to think of Matt. But like that trick where you tried not to think of a pink elephant, every effort to banish the guy into some dark corner of her mind failed. He was on stage, front and center.

She sipped her coffee, eyeing the bottom drawer under the cabinet where odd bits and pieces of stuff always ended up. She'd shoved Matt's mystery box in there, with a rubber band ball, a couple of screwdrivers and the keys from her old apartment. The slip of paper with the question mark was still inside. She didn't want to look at it. She didn't even want to think about it. But she just didn't have the heart to throw it away.

She'd given Matt her phone number Sunday before she left the gorge, just as Emma had suggested. It was only Wednesday now. Only three days later. Three days was nothing. And yet, it felt like a yawning chasm of time. In those same three days, Jake had called Emma at least a dozen times. And had texted her constantly in between. Well, of course he had. Men always called Emma.

Casey's little sister was currently holed up in the bathroom, humming as she put on her makeup. Jake had called from the train station a half hour ago; he'd be at the door any minute. He and Emma were going to a party tonight in the city, then heading back to Boston tomorrow for New Year's Eve. Jake's band was playing at some fancy hotel, and he'd insisted Emma join them as guest vocalist. Emma was thrilled.

Casey pressed a sudden throbbing pain between her eyes. Emma had, of course, interrogated Jake about Matt. Jake had returned only the vaguest answers. Emma had made excuses for Matt, but as far as Casey was concerned, there was only one conclusion to draw. If Matt was interested, he would have called. He hadn't, so he wasn't.

Casey grabbed her coat off the couch and shoved an arm into one sleeve. She had to face facts. The days—and nights—she'd spend in Dutch Gorge hadn't been real. They'd been an aberration, a pleasant interlude. The problem was that she'd allowed herself to hope the gorge's magic would follow her back to the city. It hadn't.

She flicked off the lamp, plunging the room into silent darkness. Not Dutch Gorge dark, of course. Plenty of artificial light spilled through the venetian blinds. And it wasn't all that quiet, either. The closed window only blocked the worst of the street noise.

"Casey? That you?"

Casey winced as her sister flipped on light.

"I thought I heard you get up," Emma said. "Please tell me you're not going back to the office already. You need to go right back to bed. You look awful."

"Thanks a lot."

Emma examined Casey more closely and frowned. "I mean it. Are you sick or something?"

"No. Not really. It's just a sleep-deprivation headache."

"Not surprising. Did you take something?"

"Yes," Casey lied.

"Well, what about—" The street intercom buzzed. "Oh!" Emma's face lit up. "That'll be Jake. He's early!"

Matt's brother arrived at the door half a minute later, flourishing a limp street vendor bouquet. Emma gushed as though he'd delivered an armful of hothouse orchids. She disappeared into the kitchen to put the wilted daisies and carnations in water.

"Casey," Jake said, dropping an overnight bag on the floor. "Hi."

"Hi, Jake. Good to see you."

"Good to see you, too. Hey, listen. Emma said you'd have a few free days after your New Year's Eve promo thing went down, and I was thinking... Why don't you come up to Boston on New Year's Day?"

"You're kidding, right?"

"I'm not. You can stay at Mary's—she has tons of room. Aunt Bea and Uncle Fred are there, of course, and—"

"And Matt."

"Um, well, yeah."

"Does he know about this?"

Jake looked discomfited. "No. I just thought of it, actually, while I was riding in on the train. But I know he'll be glad to see you."

Casey snorted. "I don't. Thanks for the offer, but there's no way I'm going to Boston to inflict myself on Matt."

"Hey, now. I wouldn't call it—"

"Jake, come off it. Your brother hasn't called me since I left the gorge. It's obvious that he doesn't want to see me."

"I think you're wrong about that, Casey."

Casey didn't like the way his words caused a hopeful clench of her heart. "Then why hasn't he called? He's got my number. And even if he's lost it, you've got my number."

"Yeah, well. It's...kind of complicated."

"No. It's not. It's very simple. One cell phone. Ten little numbers."

Jake shoved his hands into his pockets. "You're right, of course. Matt should've called you by now. And he should've called Emma, too."

"Emma?" Casey said just as her sister returned from the kitchen. "What does she have to do with it?"

Emma looked from Jake to Casey. "Did I hear my name? What are we talking about?"

Instead of answering, Jake pulled out his wallet and extracted a business card. "Here." He thrust the card into Emma's hand. "Matt's planning to call you next week, when he gets back to the city. But you might as well know now."

"What—?" Emma looked at the card and blinked. "Oh. My. God. No. This cannot be real."

Casey peered over her sister's shoulder. Emma's hand was trembling, making it hard to make out the printing on the card. She grabbed her sister's wrist and held it still.

Matthew Joseph
Matthew Joseph Casting Agency
Theater, Film, Advertising

Emma's hand was trembling. "Jake," she breathed. "You can't *mean* this. Matt is Matthew *Joseph?*"

"Yep," Jake said. "He is."

She let out a squeal. "*Ohmygod!* I can't believe it!"

Casey released Emma's wrist. "Who's Matthew Joseph?"

Emma was gulping in big breaths of air. "Only..." she gasped. "...one of..." *Gasp.* "...the hottest casting agents...in Manhattan!" She launched herself at Jake. "And he's really going to call me? Next week? Really?"

"Yeah," Jake said, chuckling as he caught her at the waist and spun her around once. "He really is. Matt's got a few projects coming up he thinks you'll be interested in, and—Jesus, Emma!"

He placed steadying hands on Emma's shoulders and peered down into her face. "Stop hyperventilating, for chrissakes. It's not instant stardom. A couple TV commercials. A city-wide print campaign. And maybe, if you audition well, a small role in an off-Broadway production. It's only a start—"

"It doesn't matter! I'll take anything! Anything. Oh, my *God*. Matthew Joseph. And I didn't even know. He never said a word!" She rounded on Jake. "And neither did you! I can't believe it."

"Wait a minute." Casey was lagging about three steps

behind. "Matt's last name is Van der Staappen. Isn't it?"

"His middle name is Joseph," Jake said. "He goes by Matt Joseph professionally."

"And he's a casting director?"

"Yeah. A very successful one."

"But...why all the secrecy? Why didn't he just say something to Emma at Dutch Lodge?"

Jake rocked back on his heels. "Uh...well, I'm afraid that was kinda my fault. When I found out Emma was an actress, I asked Matt to keep quiet. I was afraid she wouldn't give me the time of day if she knew who Matt was. So I asked Matt to back off, and distract you a little, while I worked on getting Emma's full attention."

"Oh, Jake," Emma exclaimed, kissing his cheek. "That is just so sweet."

"And it certainly explains a few things," Casey muttered. Specifically, why Matt hadn't called. He'd only hooked up with her as a favor to his brother. And once he got back to the city, neck deep in actresses and models, he hadn't spared her a second thought.

She'd been three kids of fool to hope it'd be anything more.

Emma seemed to have finally gotten control of herself. She turned to Casey, sympathy flashing in her eyes. "Oh, Case. I'm sure—"

"Aren't the two of you late for your party?" Casey said sharply. "I mean, it's after ten already. You better get going."

Emma sent her a worried look. "Um...we don't really

have to go, do we Jake?"

"No," Jake said promptly. "Not at all. We could hang out here tonight if you want."

"No," Casey said, heading toward the door. "Please. Go. I'm headed back to the office, and I won't be back until after deadline. We go live tomorrow night at nine."

"Well...okay," Emma said. "If you're sure you're all right."

"I'm fine," Casey said.

Chapter Eleven

Matt felt like a goddamned stalker.

What the hell was he doing in Greenwich Village, pacing up and down the sidewalk in front of Casey's apartment building? An hour to midnight on New Year's Eve, no less. He'd gotten her work number from Emma days ago. He could have called her any time—God knows he was on the phone half his life anyway. And yet he procrastinated. She was on a tight deadline, he told himself. Better to wait.

A half hour ago, though, he'd caved. Deadline or no deadline, he had to at least hear her voice and find out where he stood. But when he dialed her office, he was told by some scratchy-voiced guy that Casey had gone home at nine, right after the campaign went live. He had her home number, too. And yet, here he was.

Screw the phone. He needed to see her, face to face.

Needle-sharp sleet spit from a charcoal sky. Damn. He should've brought an umbrella. Or a hat, at least. An icy wind gusted up the street. He turned up his collar and ducked into the meager shelter of the apartment doorway.

Production title: Idiot in Love. Pathetic Romeo lurks

in a city doorway...

He located the buzzer for her apartment on a panel by the door. Taking a deep breath, he pressed it.

No answer. But she had to be there. He'd just talked to Jake; during the conversation, Emma had been texting Casey. She was home. Alone.

He buzzed again. And again, until her irritated voice came over the intercom.

"Yes?"

"Casey? It's Matt. Can I come up?"

Dead silence.

And then, "Is this Matt Van der Staappen? Or Matthew Joseph?"

He sighed. "Please. Just let me in. It's cold out here."

He heard a soft snort. "Yeah. Like you're not used to that."

A couple seconds later, though, he heard the door unlatched. He climbed the four flights and knocked at the door.

She opened it. For a long moment, they just stared at each other. His heart gave a lurch. She looked adorable, with her messy hair and flushed cheeks. Her faded jeans and rumpled sweater made him want to drag her right into bed.

Her gaze flicked over him, her expression inscrutable. He wondered what she was thinking. Casey looked like the woman he'd fallen for in Dutch Gorge, but Matt, dressed in charcoal wool dress slacks and a black turtleneck, was a far cry from the denim-and-flannel guy she'd known there.

She leaned on the jamb, one hand on the doorknob, blocking his view into the apartment.

"So," she said, crossing her arms. "What do you want?"

He shoved his hands into the pockets of his trench coat. "I know Jake told you about what I do for a living," he said. "But I wanted to explain."

She shoved a curl out of her eyes. He fought the urge to tuck it behind her ear.

When she didn't answer, he continued. "He told you why I kept my casting agency a secret in Dutch Gorge."

Her lips twisted. "Yeah. Something about keeping me out of the way while he moved in on Emma."

"It wasn't like that at all." He shoved a hand through his hair. "Well, not exactly, anyway."

"And really," she continued, "it all worked out fine. Jake's a great guy. He and Emma hit it off. And you and I...well, we got a few nights of sex. So it's all good."

She started to close the door. He put a hand on it to stop it from hitting him in the face. "Damn it Casey, that's not how it is between us, and you know it."

"No, Matt. I don't know it. I know nothing. I don't know why you worked so hard to get me into bed. I don't know why you bothered to take my number. And I don't know why you're here."

"Then let me in. Let me explain."

"That's not a good idea. I mean, what would be the point? You have your life, filled with actresses and models, and I have mine, filled with computer geeks. Believe me, I've been around enough of Emma's friends to know the two cultures just don't mix."

"I'm not going to discuss this in the hallway."

"No. Because there's nothing to discuss."

"Casey..."

With a sigh, she stepped back. "All right. Fine. Suit yourself."

He entered the apartment and closed the door firmly behind him. Turning, he found himself in a small, cluttered living room. A futon couch and matching chair flanked a coffee table in the center of the room. The potted palm by the window looked like it was in need of watering. A bookshelf crowded with software and computer game boxes half-shielded a computer desk, where an oversized monitor fought for desk space with a collection of empty cola cans.

A flat-screen TV on the wall was tuned to coverage of New Year's Eve festivities on Times Square. Casey's laptop was open on the coffee table, nestled amid fashion magazines and empty coffee cups, flashing photo after photo of passionate kisses. Underneath, the vote tally for each couple rose.

"Your project?" he asked. "The Most Romantic Kiss contest? How's it going?"

"Fantastic. It rolled out like clockwork, and the response is tremendous."

"That's great."

"I guess." Taking a seat on the futon, she punched the mute on the remote. "Okay, get on with it. Why are you here?"

Now that she was asking, and waiting for an answer, Matt wondered if anything he said now would make a difference. Shrugging out of his coat, he turned and hung it on a coat stand by the door. Dropping into the chair on Casey's right, he rested his forearms on his thighs and stared at his clasped hands.

"I guess you wondered why I didn't call."

He slid a glance at her, but she wasn't looking at him. Her eyes were trained on her computer. A photo of a couple kissing on a tropical beach faded into a picture of a couple lip-locked in front of a massive barbeque grill.

"The question might have crossed my mind," she said quietly.

"I drove out to Boston from Dutch Gorge on Sunday. I just got back to Manhattan today."

"There's cell reception all over New England. Or so I've heard."

"Yeah, I know. I thought about calling. Constantly, in fact. But...I don't know. It didn't seem right. I wanted to see you. But at the same time, I was afraid when I saw you it would be too...different, I guess. Awkward."

She didn't reply.

He exhaled and continued. "Awkward, like it is right now. I didn't know what you'd think of the man I am here in the city. I'm not exactly who I pretended to be upstate."

"Why pretend at all?" She finally looked at him. "That's what I don't understand. Why didn't you just tell me who you were?"

"At first, I kept quiet for Jake. So he could get to know

Emma without me and my agency as a distraction." He shrugged. "Sounds conceited, I know."

She snorted. "No. It sounds realistic. Jake was right. If Emma had known who you were, Jake would have become instantly invisible." Her gaze skittered away. "You must know hundreds of women as beautiful and as talented as Emma in your business."

"I suppose I do," he said carefully. "But truthfully? They all blur together after a while. Not one of them stands out. Not like you do."

"Oh, please."

"I'm serious, Casey. You got my attention that first moment in the parking lot, when you fell into my arms. And then later, when I was getting your luggage?" He chuckled. "Man, you were so pissed at Emma. I could practically see the smoke coming out of your ears."

She shot him a look of pure incredulity. "So, you're trying to tell me you were attracted by my clumsiness and bad temper?"

He gave a wry laugh. "Honestly? I think it was more the fact that you weren't trying to impress me. You have no idea how appealing that was. But then, the more time I spent with you, the more I liked you. I can't tell you how glad I was that Emma kept locking you out of your room."

"But...why didn't you tell me about your work then? I wouldn't have told Emma until the weekend was over, if you'd asked me to keep quiet. But you never mentioned a word about being a casting director. You didn't even tell me you lived in Manhattan. Why not?"

"It's...hard to explain. In Dutch Gorge, the real world seems so far away, and I like it that way. I didn't feel like talking about my career, answering all the usual questions. And you didn't seem to have a very high opinion of the business anyway." He sighed. "Don't get me wrong, I love what I do. But last weekend, I just wanted a break from...everything. I found myself wanting to be the man I might have been if I hadn't left the gorge. Just for a few days, anyway."

He rubbed a hand down his face. "Does any of that make any kind of sense?"

"A little, I suppose." She tucked her legs under her and looped her arms around her knees. "Dutch Gorge made me want to be someone different, too. Someone more...uninhibited, I guess. Like Emma."

"Once I got to Boston," he said slowly, "what we shared in the gorge...it seemed like a dream. Like it hadn't really happened."

"I felt the same way," Casey murmured. "Even when it was happening. At first, I couldn't believe you were sincere. I kept thinking it couldn't last. And then, when you didn't call..."

"I didn't call because I didn't know what to say. At least, not over the phone. I only knew what I wanted to tell when I saw you again."

"And what was that?"

He took a deep breath and put his heart on the line. "That maybe last weekend showed both of us who we really are. And I wanted to ask if you thought we could find a way to keep some of that Dutch Gorge Christmas magic alive here in the city. All year long. Despite all the distractions and stress of the real world. What do you say, Casey?" He brushed a curl off her forehead. "Do you think we could work? Even with our lives plugged in?"

For a long moment, he thought she wasn't going to answer. Her expression was as serious as he'd ever seen it. She stared at the kissing couples on the laptop screen— waterfall, museum, desert. Twin furrows dug between her brows. He could almost hear the wheels turning in her head.

Then she drew a breath, and met his eyes. "I don't know if that will work," she said. "But..."

The tight knot in Matt's chest eased.

"But if you want to give it a try..." She trailed off again.

"I do." He said quickly.

She smiled. "Then I do, too."

He answered with a grin of his own. "Hallelujah."

He glanced up at the TV. It was one minute to midnight. "And just in time for the New Year, too."

Casey leaned forward and studied her computer. "We're down to the last two kisses" One was shot on a mountaintop. The other was taken in mid-air, of kissing skydivers.

"One of those couples is going to Paris," Casey said. Then, to Matt's surprise, she hit the power button.

The computer went dark. On the TV, the Times Square crystal ball began to drop, countdown numbers flashing. *Eight...seven...six...five...*

Reaching over the coffee table, Casey punched the off button on the remote, too. The apartment plunged into darkness.

"What are you doing?" Matt asked. "You worked on this project for weeks. Don't you want to know who wins?"

Her outline was a blur, illuminated only by the light streaming through the half-closed Venetian blinds. She rose from the futon; her warm body slipped into his lap.

His arms tightened around her as the peppershot of firecrackers exploded in the street.

She nuzzled his cheek. "I don't need to watch," she said. "I already know which couple's won."

When she kissed him, he knew, too.

Thank You

Thank you for reading *Christmas Unplugged*. I hope you enjoyed it! Would you like to know when my next book is available? There are a few ways you can keep in touch:

Sign up for my monthly newsletter
at joynash.com

Visit me on social media
facebook.com/joynash/
twitter: @sunflowerM0M
joynash.blogspot.com

Happy Reading!

Turn the page to read an excerpt from

Looking for a Hero
Available Now!

joynash.com
excerpts, extras,
behind-the-book secrets

Looking for a Hero

by Joy Nash

When supervillain Lex Loser threatens the world with a computerized neutron bomb, Heroes United for Freedom turns to its least likely hero to save the day.

Excerpt

Wednesday, 10:47 PM
Three days, one hour, thirteen minutes, and counting...

Oh, man. It was his lucky day. An original 1951 Action Comics #158, The Kid from Krypton, shimmered enticingly, nineteen minutes from closing on eBay.

Yes! Clark Kendall raised both arms in a two-fisted salute to the superhero gods. He'd lusted after this particular Superman comic book for ages. Now it was as good as his.

He typed in his bid the old-fashioned way: on his laptop keyboard. It launched into cyberspace just as he became aware of the sound of a chirping bird, followed by the drone of an airplane, coming from the cordless phone at his elbow. He made a point of reprogramming the office ringtone whenever he was on desk duty.

He hit the answer button. "Heroes United For Freedom... Yeah, we deliver... Go ahead..."

He shifted the phone to one shoulder as he watched the eBay screen refresh. "One roast beef hero sandwich, no onions... one Italian hero, hold the mayo... Drinks with that?... Two Cokes... Your address?... Right. Got it. Twenty minutes."

He cut the connection, wondering how long it would be before the hungry customers figured out their dinner wasn't coming. It was amazing, really. Somehow, even with absolutely no advertising and an unlisted phone number, the fake New York-style sub shop four levels above his head still managed to attract business. It almost made him want to open a take-out joint in Newark, New Jersey for real.

Almost, but not quite.

He pushed his glasses up the bridge of his nose and squinted at the laptop screen. Damn. Someone had topped his bid. He typed in a counter offer and sent it scurrying across the broadband connection.

"Hey, Clark."

He swiveled his chair toward the door, swallowing hard. Diana Price had come looking for him? More luck. That only happened in his dreams.

He held his breath as the shapely Amazonian princess sashay the HUFF control room, forty-four-and-a-half double D's all but exploding from her star spangled corset. When she leaned over the back of his chair and brushed her breasts against his shoulders, he nearly turned blue and passed out.

"What'cha doing?" she asked, leaning over his shoulder. Her breath tickled his ear.

Trying desperately to breathe, Clark thought, but masculine pride prevented him from announcing that little bit of information.

"I'm on eBay," he told her. "I put in a bid on a Superman comic book."

"Think you'll get it?"

He twisted his neck, angling for a better view of her boobs without being too obvious. Did he think he'd get it? From Diana? No, but a man could dream.

"Clark? You okay?"

He gave himself a mental shake. "Yeah, fine. Listen," he said, forcing a casual tone. "My shift's almost done. You want to go out for a drink afterward?"

Diana's red lips quirked knowingly at him. Too knowingly. He knew he was toast even before she started laughing.

"I can't." She presented him a smile reserved for children, puppies, and guys who were about to get the shaft. "I've got a date with Bruce."

Clark's fist closed on the computer mouse so tightly it was a wonder the thing didn't let out a squeal. Bruce Wynn, superhero. Scratch that. Superjerk.

"He's just using you for sex," Clark said.

Diana only laughed. "I know! That's what makes it fun." She gave him a little hug. "Aw, Clark, are you jealous? That's so sweet."

He felt his cheeks heat. Sweet. Yeah, just what every superhero aspired to.

As if on cue, Bruce appeared at the door, arms crossed over his steroid-enhanced chest. Muscles bulged under his gray spandex shirt and black tights. He wasn't wearing his cape at the moment, but Clark could almost see the shiny black fabric flapping in an imaginary breeze.

Bruce gave an infinitesimal nod in Diana's general direction. "Babe." His moody gaze shifted the tiniest bit to the right. "Clark."

Diana rushed across the room, gushing a reply. Clark's stomach turned slightly nauseous. Sure, Bruce was something to look at—and if you believed half the rumors, a veritable god in bed—but was that all a woman wanted in a guy? You'd think rock hard abs, a perfect profile, and a bottomless supply of gloomy angst would get old after a while.

Bruce and Diana melded into a liplock. Clark pushed his glasses up the bridge of his nose and turned back to eBay. Only two minutes left, and he'd been knocked off the top again. Hell. He upped his bid into four figures and sent it flying. No way was he going to let this one go.

The phone rang again.

"Heroes United For Freedom," Clark droned, then snapped to attention when Captain Marvelous' radio announcer baritone boomed across the line.

"Clark, round up the troops. We've got a situation."

"A situation, Captain?"

From the corner of his eye, he saw Bruce and Diana disengage.

"Can't say any more on an unsecured line, son, but I can tell you the outlook is not good. Not good at all."

Was it ever?

"Tell every hero we've got on the books to report to my

ready room in one hour."

Whoa. Clark couldn't remember the last time The Captain had ordered a full HUFF assembly. This was major. A dire threat to life as they all knew it, most likely.

His gaze drifted back to eBay. Damn. His mysterious opponent had topped his bid two seconds before the countdown expired. The Kid from Krypton was history.

It looked like Clark's luck had run out.

Wednesday, 11:00 PM
Three days, one hour, and counting...

Yes!

Blossom Breeze sprang to her feet and did a little victory dance around her chair. That last minute bidder had come out of nowhere. She'd practically broken out in a cold sweat, but somehow she managed to squeak in under the wire to win the eBay bid for Action Comics #158, *The Kid from Krypton*. She'd only been looking for that particular issue *forever*. After it was framed, she'd hang it on her wall right between her signed portraits of Christopher Reeve and Dean Cain.

She collapsed in her chair and beamed at the screen. Life was perfect.

A nanosecond later, a chat message popped up on her screen.

<Hey, Blossom>

Bernie. Okay, well maybe life wasn't completely perfect.

<Hey, Bernie> she typed back, mentally adding the emoticon for rolling eyes. Bernie was sitting on the other side of the cubicle partition on her left, less than five feet away.

Another geek occupied the cubicle to her right. Oh, sure, she could put a positive spin on things and say she spent every night surrounded by single men under thirty, but where would that get her? She'd still be right here in the computer lab at Megalopolis Polytechnic Institute.

She sighed as a series of numbers materialized in her chat window. Another one of Bernie's freaking mathematical cryptograms. A second later, his head popped up over the partition, all bright eyes and big ears.

"Well, what do you say?"

Blossom squinted at Bernie's coded message, but it was late, and it'd been a tough day. The encryption could've spelled out "Do you want to get naked?" and she wouldn't even have known.

Hey. Wait a minute...

She blinked at the screen, mentally decoding: *Do you want to...*

A sudden vision of a naked Bernie seared her brain, doing instant damage to all major synapses. Oh, please. No. Anything but that. Bernie weighed all of one hundred and thirty pounds, soaking wet. Naked or clothed, no thank you.

Tentatively, she deciphered the rest of the code. *...go to the Star Trek convention tomorrow?*

Her breath left in a rush. Thank you, God.

"So? Do you?" Bernie's goofy grin stretched from ear

to ear, his tongue lolling out of his mouth, puppy dog style. No doubt he thought encrypted chat message propositioning a very clever way to procure female companionship.

"Brent Spiner's going to be there," he said in a wheedling tone.

Blossom gave him a thin smile. "I'd love to, Bernie. I really would. But tomorrow's not good for me." She had to feed her goldfish. And wash her hair. And visit her gynecologist. "Maybe some other time."

"Geez, that's too bad. A bunch of us are going to my place afterwards for a TNG marathon."

TNG, Blossom knew only too well, was Geekspeak for *Star Trek, The Next Generation.* As in Picard, Data, Geordie and the gang.

"Sorry. I'll have to pass."

"Your loss," Bernie said, and ducked back into his cell.

Sighing, Blossom logged off and shut down. Bernie wasn't a bad guy, really. You could even make the case that his brain made up for what he lacked in physique. Of course, that was pretty much true of all the guys lurking in the bowels of the MPI computer department.

Call her shallow, but Blossom just couldn't seem to get past appearances when it came to men. She preferred guys with muscles. Lots of muscles, bulging out all over. She drooled over sculpted pecs and corded biceps. She spun elaborate fantasies starring hunk who looked like the superheroes on her apartment walls.

Which could only be termed an ironic twist of fate, since Blossom's off-the-charts IQ and meticulous coding talents had dumped her squarely into geekdom. In her world, men who fit the superhero mold were very few and extremely far between.

Wasn't life a bitch?

About the Author

Joy Nash is a USA Today Bestselling Author and RITA Award Finalist applauded by Booklist for her "tart wit, superbly crafted characters, and sexy, magic-steeped plots."

When Joy was seven years old, she read a book about a girl who lived on the moon. She thought it was real until her big sister came along and messed up the story with the truth. Ever since, Joy's been of the opinion that fiction is way more interesting than reality. She credits her love of tortured heroes to the Brontë sisters, her fascination with magical adventure to J.R.R. Tolkien, and her weakness for snarky humor to Douglas Adams.

Connect with Joy
facebook.com/joynash/
twitter: @joynashauthor
joynash.blogspot.com

May the stories never end!

www.ingramcontent.com/pod-product-compliance
Lightning Source LLC
Chambersburg PA
CBHW060617130626
46555CB00002B/538